Reincarnation

REINCARNATION

An Historical Novel Spanning 4,000 Years

Michael J. Lowis

RESOURCE *Publications* · Eugene, Oregon

REINCARNATION
An Historical Novel Spanning 4,000 Years

Resource Publications
An Imprint of Wipf and Stock Publishers
199 W. 8th Ave., Suite 3
Eugene, OR 97401

www.wipfandstock.com

PAPERBACK ISBN: 978-1-5326-4757-4
HARDCOVER ISBN: 978-1-5326-4758-1
EBOOK ISBN: 978-1-5326-4759-8

Manufactured in the U.S.A.   02/13/18

Contents

PREFACE

Maybe it is over-optimistic to decide to write about a man who lived four thousand years ago, and then expect there to be a lot of information about him. Perhaps one might have some success with Egyptian pharaohs, who made sure their exploits were recorded in hieroglyphics for posterity. But few other individuals would have had this privilege, and such details we do have about early historical figures were often preserved through oral tradition for hundreds of years before being written down.

And we all know what can happen to accuracy when a message is verbally passed from person to person!

Nevertheless, challenges are there to be grasped, not avoided, so this is the story of Melchizedek who, we are led to believe, lived about 2,000 BCE. He is mentioned only very briefly in three places in the Christian Bible. The fact that these references to him were included by those who compiled the Canon, suggests that he was acknowledged to have been a real—and significant—person. Of course, we cannot regard this as a certainty, although his name also crops up in other ancient writings that remain apocryphal, including the Dead Sea Scrolls, the Gnostic Gospels discovered in Egypt, *The Book of the Secrets of Enoch*, and in various Jewish oral and written traditions.

Despite the sparsity of information available, the intention was always to try and underpin this story with evidence from whatever historical accounts exist, even if they were more concerned with myths and legends than with authenticated facts. To mention just one example, whilst the opening passages may seem to stretch credibility, they reflect what has been written in ancient documents. The sources consulted for this and other events related in the narrative have been compiled in an Appendix. Small superscript numbers have been added to the text to indicate where documentary sources have been drawn upon to help enhance its authenticity. These can be ignored without jeopardizing the reading enjoyment, but they will enable readers who are interested in finding out more about any particular aspect of the account, to be able to locate the source material for themselves.

Many aspects of the story have been dramatized or fictionalized, in order to provide continuity. This includes the notion of reincarnation itself but, even here, there is an underpinning of scientific and psychological theory.

Thus, dear reader, enjoy this tale of the intriguing historical figure of Melchizedek.

Regard it as pure fantasy if you wish—or maybe it will provide you with a little food for thought. Hmm, perhaps it really could have happened?

THE BEGINNING

Mel awoke. Or at least he thought he was awake. Something seemed strange and unfamiliar, yet not completely alien. He tried to look around, but there was only darkness. He tried to move, but could only shift his limbs and body a centimeter or two by pushing against the slightly-yielding cocoon that surrounded him. Despite this, he felt warm and protected and, somewhat to his surprise, not on the verge of a panic attack.

Unable to deduce where he was and what he was doing, Mel thought it might become clear if he could attract somebody's attention. He tried to shout: "Is anybody there?"

Although he mouthed the words, no sound emerged. Only then did he realize that he was not actually breathing. With an effort, he managed to suppress the feelings of terror that were starting to invade him, and made a first stab at an explanation. Could I be dead? He wondered if this was what it would be like when you shed your mortal coil, and commenced the journey to whatever lay beyond. If so, and despite his apprehension, it was still not unbearable—at least for the moment.

But the death explanation was probably unlikely. He remembered going home the previous night, after a very enjoyable

dinner party with friends to celebrate his engagement to Angelina, his childhood sweetheart. It had been a Saturday, and they
had swapped jokes, philosophized about the meaning of life, and
imbibed just a tad too much wine. It was nearly midnight when the
taxi dropped Mel off at his bachelor flat, and he was glad to retire
to bed soon afterwards, soporific from the effects of one glass too
many. Sleep had beckoned, and he had no desire to resist.

Ah, that's the answer, Mel said to himself. I am having a lucid
dream, one of those rare occasions when you are aware that you
are dreaming but do not wake up. I know that sleep paralysis stops
a person moving and, because of this, some folk even think they
are being abducted by aliens. If this is the case, then I shall just
relax and let the dream play itself out. Soon I shall wake up, and
any memory of this will quickly fade away and be forgotten.

But there was just one thing that did not quite fit this picture.
He became aware of a regular, pulsing sound all around him and, if
he concentrated hard, he was sure he could hear indistinct voices.
Where on earth was he—assuming it was actually on this earth?

Then, all at once, two things started to happen. Mel felt him
self slowly starting to move, head first, as if he were being squeezed
along a tunnel. At the same time, one of the voices became a little
louder and more distinct. It was a man speaking, and he could
just make out the words, "Rest for a moment now, Sopanima; you
can try again shortly." The movement stopped. Who was this 'Sopanima', and what was she doing? he asked himself.

A minute or two passed and there was another voice, from
a woman this time, and so loud that it seemed to resonate from
the very fabric that surrounded him. There were no words, just
one long drawn-out cry of, "Ahhhhh." Silence followed, and even
the pulsing sound that he had been hearing came to a stop. After a
pause, the man now spoke again: "Alas, it looks like Sopanima has
now departed; we shall have to complete this job by ourselves, Nir."
Mel was aware that he had been gripped by the head and was being
gently pulled along the tunnel.

He felt the soft walls around him gradually starting to lose
resistance. Suddenly his head was free, and he took his first gulp

of fresh air. Moments later his arms were also out in the open, and then his legs. Had he just been rescued after being trapped after some sort of disaster? If so, it was wonderful to be liberated; he must face his rescuers and thank them for their valiant efforts.

It took a little time for the reality of the situation to dawn on him. Mel looked around the room, at his 'rescuers', then at what he had been 'rescued' from. There could only be one possible explanation: he had just been born!

Chapter I

THE REBIRTH

Mel's mind was swirling with confusion, and he felt the icy finger of terror starting to run down his spine. He was already a grown man, just turned thirty years old, with a job, friends, and a fiancée whom he was due to marry in the not too distant future.

Yes, during the previous night's dinner party, the conversation had dwelt for a time on the idea of reincarnation. They knew that Buddhism and Hinduism were among those religions that believed in the transmigration of the soul. What you came back as in a future life depended on how you had lived in the present one. If you had been good, then you might be reborn as a person who would achieve great things, but bad boys and girls could come back as lowly animals or maybe even trees.

They had enjoyed speculating about what sort of creature each of them deserved to be, but nobody took this idea seriously. It was no joking matter now; could it be that he had died and was being reincarnated in another body?

Whilst struggling to accept that such a rebirth could even be a remote possibility, Mel thought that it might help to take a closer look at just where he was now. He was slightly buoyed by the notion that it could even be interesting if he had returned at some point in the future, and there were some exciting new scientific developments to experience. However, what he saw did nothing to confirm this possibility. By the light of flickering oil lamps he could see two middle-aged men, each wearing a white robe that was secured at the waist with a colored sash. On their feet were simple, brown leather sandals. He had to crane his neck upwards to see their bearded faces. Looking down at his own body, he could see that he was similarly clothed, but he was only the height of a small child.

This certainly did not appear to be the future, but more likely the past, and the distant past at that. Surely this is not how re-incarnation, if this was indeed the explanation, was supposed to work. Or was it? Can time go backwards? he asked himself. Mel had always been fascinated by what the cosmologists had to say about time travel, although it was often very difficult to grasp. He recalled once hearing that there was something about the speed of light, time warps, and wormholes, that made travelling back in time theoretically possible, all based on Einstein's Theory of Relativity.[1] But could this also apply to the transmigration of souls? Maybe such spirits were not constrained by the same scientific laws as was physical matter.

Leaving this question unanswered, Mel turned around and saw the lifeless form of an elderly woman lying on a bed. Confusion reigned once more in his mind. If she was his mother, and he had just been born, presumably with the help of the two males—for he could see no others in the room—then how was he now standing there as a boy of about three years old, wearing clothing, and able to think like the adult he still felt himself to be? A wave of sadness overcame him; this poor soul who had apparently borne him had not lived to see her son enter this world. He climbed up onto the bed and sat by her side.

One of the men then spoke. "I am Nir, your father." Indicating to the other man, he added, "This is your uncle Noah, who is my brother."[2] I have heard of Noah, Mel said to himself; if this is the same man, then he is a famous figure from the ancient Hebrew

Scriptures. But does this mean that I have been reborn to a time at least two thousand years before Jesus took his first steps on earth? His thoughts were interrupted when Nir continued: "Your mother, Sopanima, died before she could complete giving birth to you, so your uncle and I had to deliver you ourselves." Then came an even more startling statement: "Although I am your earthly father, your mother was a virgin. I have several wives, but I had not slept with Sopanima; no man had. I do not know how she conceived, but there are many things in this life that we do not understand."

Just as he thought he was beginning to form an understanding of the situation in which he now found himself, Mel started to become seriously concerned. He knew of only one person who was reported to have had a virgin birth and, if his suspicions were correct, it would be two millennia before that man would be born. Surely, he asked himself, there could not be any connection between that great prophet and himself.

Leaving this frightening possibility aside for the moment, Mel wondered if, in his infant state, he had yet developed the ability to speak in a comprehensible way. He tentatively experimented by asking a question, and was encouraged by the confident and mature tone of the voice that came from his mouth. "Where is this place?" he said.

"We are in the land of Mesopotamia," Nir replied. "The River Nile is to the west of us, and the Euphrates and Tigris are to the east." He continued, "Great things are expected of you, my son. For this reason, you shall be named Melchizedek, which means 'King of Righteousness'. Not only have you been born as a well-developed child, rather than a helpless baby, but you have the Badge of Priesthood on your breast." [3]

Mel looked down. There was no badge on his tunic, so he pulled the garment open. Horrified, he saw that his chest was covered in scales, like those of a serpent! "Am I half snake and half human?" he shrieked.

"No," Nir said. "Please do not be distressed. This is a sign given by El Elyon, our one god, to very few people, and it shows that you have been chosen for a special mission. Sometimes horns and a tail are also present." Frantically, Mel probed his body but he could not feel any evidence of these unwelcome appendages—at least not yet!

Nir was speaking again. "Our Lord is displeased with the way folk are turning away from him, and he has threatened to send a disaster that will kill all but a faithful few." After a short pause, he continued, "Your uncle, Noah, along with his family, is among those who will be spared, and this will now include you so that you will be able to complete your appointed task on earth."

Mel struggled to assimilate all this information, but it did confirm his earlier suspicion regarding the era in which he had been reborn. If this was the same Noah whose story is narrated in the Scriptures, then the threatened disaster would be the great flood. It must indeed be around two thousand years before the start of what would be known as the Christian Era. But what was this 'special mission' he was destined to fulfill? In due course, he would find out.

Chapter 2

THE ARK

Not only had Mel (for he preferred to retain that name rather than the more cumbersome Melchizedek) emerged into the world as a young boy rather than a baby, but he was also aging unnaturally quickly. Nir, his brother Noah, and his three sons Shem, Ham, and Japheth, had taken him into their care and nurtured him, but he seemed to have little need to rely on earthly sustenance. Regardless of how little food he ate, he rapidly grew into a strong young man.

His main concern was to try and understand what he was destined to achieve in this life into which he had been unwillingly transported. The only response he received when he tried to question the men about this was, "We are not the ones to know the answer to this, but El Elyon will tell you in his own good time." Frustrating though this was, Mel had no option but to wait and see. Nevertheless, it was unsettling when he was regarded by everyone as someone special, but was not able to respond to this reverence in any meaningful way.

The men were busy every day for as long as the sun gave light, building a large wooden ship. Mel learned a lot about carpentry through both watching and helping the others, although his own contributions were mainly restricted to unskilled tasks such as fetching, carrying, and holding the rough planks of wood steady whilst the adults used saws or chisels to fashion them into shape. The family did not live next to the sea or a major river but, whenever he asked why they were building such a large sailing vessel on dry land, the answer was, "We are doing what the Lord has bidden us to do; we shall find out the reason for this when he wishes to tell us."

There was something else that added to Mel's already confused state of mind; it was that Noah was apparently five hundred years old. Nir had told him this during one of their conversations, when he was trying to find out more about the situation into which he had been transported. "How can this be true?" he had asked. "You and your brother appear to be of similar age, but you tell me that you have only reached one tenth of Noah's longevity." He wondered if there could be a system in use for measuring age that was different from that with which he was familiar. Nir's reply was so preposterous that it did little to resolve this conjecture.

"We come from an extended line of long-lived people, but only the first son in each generation has this ability." Urged on my Mel to give more details, Nir said, "First there was Adam, and he lived to be nine-hundred and thirty years. His son was Seth, who also exceeded nine-hundred years, as did Seth's own son Enosh, and his boy Kenan." He continued, "Five generations later, Lamech, the father of Noah and me, died at the age of seven-hundred and seventy-seven years. Thus, it is not surprising that my brother is only just into his extended middle-age." [4]

A more satisfying explanation was clearly not going to be offered so, for the present, Mel just had to accept what Nir had told him. However, he did ask, "Aren't you jealous that you, not being the first-born son, will not be granted the same privilege of such a long life?"

"I shall accept whatever time I am allotted," Nir replied. But what Mel heard next severely dented his already fragile psyche: "But you, Melchizedek, will live for ever!" And with that, the discussion on this topic came to an end, and was never mentioned again.

The daily routine differed little, and the weeks rolled by. The ark, for that is what the adults were now calling the vessel, gradually neared completion. Noah had said to him, "This ship will be a place of protection, a refuge for my family and me, as well as for some other creatures." He continued, "A great catastrophe will occur soon, and this will destroy the world with which we are familiar."

"How long will I be on the ship?" Mel had asked.

"You will not be joining us," was Noah's reply.

"But I thought you said that you and your family would be safe on the ark," Mel bleated out, in a state of agitation. "Surely I am now a part of your family." Reassurance came quickly.

"Never fear, my nephew, you are a special one, and will be protected in a special way." Again, Mel had to be content with such a vague response, as no further details were forthcoming, despite his attempts to probe further.

It became noticeable that the weather was starting to change. Instead of the bright and sunny days to which Mel had grown accustomed, there was now an increasing amount of cloud cover. It was obvious that the sky was becoming ever darker and more menacing with each passing day. Sometimes he could hear the sound of distant thunder, which suggested that rain was falling in some far-off places, although it was yet to reach his current location.

The day soon came when Noah made an announcement. He said, "El Elyon has spoken to me, and given me instructions." This is what they were all waiting for, and were keen to hear the details. "The ark has been completed, and we must now stock it with provisions. These will not be just for ourselves, but for the animals that we shall take with us. The food we gather will need to be sufficient to last us for a year."

There was thus no time to relax after all the hard work of building the vessel. Everyone, including Mel, busied themselves by gathering and preparing all the food and other items they would need, and stowing it on board the ark. No sooner was this done, than Noah pronounced: "Our Lord has again communicated with me, saying that in seven days time he will send rain, and that we and the animals have to be on the boat by then." Once again it was a case of the whole family working together to accomplish the task.

At long last, the animals had been rounded up and pairs of each species were led onto the ark and into their allotted places. The seventh day arrived; it was time for the family to leave their home for the last time, and prepare themselves for a year's residence on the boat. All but Mel, that is, as it had been made clear to him that he would be cared for in a different way. It was a tearful farewell when at last his father Nir, Uncle Noah, their wives, and his cousins Shem, Ham, and Japheth, along with their own families, boarded the vessel and raised the gangplank. Nir's last words to him were to have no fear, but just to trust that El Elyon would provide all of his needs.

Yes, Mel would try to be brave. It nevertheless seemed strange to see this massive wooden boat, stocked with animals, people, and provisions, standing there in the field with no water in sight. He went into the now deserted house where he had been born, and busied himself preparing the final meal that had been left for him. When it was dark, he lay down to sleep. The last thing he noticed before drifting into oblivion was that the sound of thunder was growing much louder, and was that the noise of raindrops splattering on the roof he could hear?

Chapter 3

THE ARCHANGEL

"Melchizedek, wake up! It is time to go." Mel was suddenly jolted out of his slumbers, to see a figure dressed all in white standing by his bed. His large wings were folded neatly around his shoulders. "I am the Archangel Michael, the one who protects the righteous. The Lord has instructed me to take you to a safe place whilst he wreaks havoc on the world, in order to punish the people for their sins."

"Where are we going?" asked Mel, in a voice still bleary after this abrupt interruption of his sleep.

"We are going to the land of Eden," said Michael. "There is a garden there that will supply all your needs until the punishment time is over. After that you will be able to continue with your mission." [5; 6]

Many questions once again raced through Mel's mind. He was again tempted to ask what this mission was that keeps being mentioned, but he suspected that an answer would still not be forthcoming. Instead he said, "How far is this place, and how will we be transported there?" Perhaps he was too optimistic in thinking that he would receive a straight-forward answer.

"We are going south, about five hundred kilometers, beyond where the Euphrates River joins the Tigris, Pishon, and Gihon. There, in the land of Eden, is an oasis set in a dry river valley.[7] You will be able to gather food from what is growing in that fertile place, and drink fresh water from the streams that trickle into the central pool; you will lack nothing."

Michael then turned to the second question. "I shall carry you on my back, and my wings will take us there. The journey can take a long time, or it can be completed in an instant, just as you wish." When asked how this could be possible, the archangel responded, "I am not constrained by the laws that have to be obeyed by people on this earth; I can be anywhere at any time in order to perform the duties assigned to me."

There seemed to be little purpose in delaying the departure any longer, so Mel said, "I shall trust you to take us there safely. But let us take sufficient time over the journey so that we can see what is happening to the world below. I have been told that The Lord is sending a disaster to destroy those who have turned away from him."

"Very well, I shall do as you ask," said the archangel. With that he let Mel climb upon his back, unfolded his magnificent wings, and gently started to rise up into the air.

Despite the rain that was now hurtling ferociously down, they did not appear to be getting wet. They flew low over the ark, and Mel could see some of his family on the deck. He waved and shouted to them as loud as he could, but nobody looked up and returned his greeting. "They cannot see or hear you," said Michael. "I am only visible to those to whom I wish to show myself. Because I am carrying you, you too are invisible."

They were soon above the mighty Euphrates River, which was already starting to overflow its banks. If the rain continued, then surely the whole land will be flooded. Before Mel could convey this thought to his companion, Michael said, "The rain will continue unabated for forty days and nights. A large area of the earth will be covered in water to a great depth, and all creatures living there will perish, except for those in the ark that Noah and his family have built."

Mel felt sadness in his heart that such terrible destruction was being inflicted on the world. But his contemplation was quickly interrupted. "We are now above the confluence of the four rivers," observed the Archangel, pointing downwards. "In a short time, we shall arrive at the Garden of Eden. This is a place that will be safe from the flood."

"I still see the land," said Mel. "But surely we should now be over the Persian Gulf?"

"This is a dry valley," Michael replied. "But one day the sea level will rise and burst over the land. It will then become the arm of the ocean of which you speak."

They had now left the rain behind them. It was still night time, but the moon shone brightly, illuminating the land below in its silvery glow. The verdant pasture that was to be their destination soon came into view. So far as Mel could tell, it appeared to be a lush haven set in the midst of an arid land that the flood had not yet reached. Amidst the trees, he could see the glinting reflection of the oasis of life-sustaining water that had welled-up from the desert floor. He had viewed and admired many paintings by artists who had imagined what the Garden of Eden was like, and was now eager to compare these with the reality that would soon be his home.

The pair gently came to rest close to a small stream. Michael said, "This will be where you will remain for the next year. If you are diligent, you will find everything you need to sustain you during this time. Before I depart, I shall tell you what your mission will be, once you are able to leave this place."

"At last," said Mel. "I have struggled to learn the reason why I am here, but nobody has yet been able to tell me."

"This information can only come from a messenger of our Lord, El Elyon. I have been instructed to inform you that you will go to the city of Salem that has been built by the Canaanites. There you will become both King and High Priest, and you will dedicate yourself to delivering the people from the power of evil."

Mel thought for a moment. Salem, was this not an early name for Jerusalem? [8] He was once again starting to feel a sense of unease. "But I have had no training in either of these roles. How can I lead and counsel others, when I am so ignorant myself?"

The reassuring voice of the archangel brought only slight relief. "You will become a messenger like me, and receive all the instruction and guidance you need from El Elyon. By the time you leave this garden, you will be a fully-developed man."

Many other questions flooded into Mel's mind, but his companion declined to give any more information. All he did was repeat that Mel should not be concerned; he would receive help and direction when it was needed.

Michael's final act was to present Mel with an ornate knife, stating, "You will be able to use this to fashion whatever tools you require, and to help harvest and prepare your food." And with that, the Archangel departed, leaving Mel alone in this bountiful place. He was glad to have the gift, and it gave him some comfort to know that it might even be needed as a weapon. The curved blade was of burnished bronze, and the sheath into which it fitted was richly decorated with red, green, and blue polished stones.

It was only now that his angelic companion had left him that Mel realized just how tired he was. His earlier slumbers had been interrupted by Michael, and it was not yet dawn. He welcomed the opportunity to lie down on a grassy bank under the stars, to try and complete his night's rest.

Sleep came quickly, but the dreams soon began. There was his fiancée Angelina, and there they were, walking hand-in-hand along the beach during their holiday last summer on the island of Guernsey. This is where he had proposed to her. She had accepted, and the next morning they visited the local jeweler to buy the engagement ring. Angelina had chosen one set with diamonds and sapphires, but they had to wait until the following day to collect it, so that the size could be adjusted to fit her slender finger. Having to pay import duty at the customs office when they returned home took the last of Mel's savings, but he had accepted this with good grace.

His fiancée had proudly shown off the ring to her friends at the office where she worked, when she returned there after the holiday. They had not immediately set a wedding date, but had agreed that it would be in about a year's time. By then Mel should have completed his architectural internship, and be earning enough money to invest in their first home. The dream continued. He and Angelina were strolling along the high street, looking in shop windows to help generate some ideas about what furniture they would like to buy, once they had their own home.

Angelina moved a few steps ahead of him. He tried to catch up, but the distance between them just kept increasing. "Stop, wait for me," he shouted, but she either did not hear, or chose not to answer him. His feet were leaden; he was losing her. Soon she was only a distant speck, and then she was gone. He felt pain and anguish; despite the many people passing by, he was alone.

Chapter 4

THE GARDEN

The first rays of the morning sun caused Mel to wake up with a start. He lay where he was, trying to gather his thoughts. It was becoming difficult to separate dreams from reality, but he came to the conclusion that he had just experienced a nightmare, triggered by the emotion of what was happening to him. He certainly missed Angelina, and wondered what the situation was in the life he had left behind. Had his absence been discovered? Had years gone by? Had Angelina presumed he had run away, and then married someone else? Oh, how he yearned for her, and longed that she could be with him now. Even in this existence, one that he had not chosen for himself, he would gladly do his best to carry out his appointed mission if only she were here by his side.

Although Mel was interested in space science and the fascinating theories that physicists announced to the world from time to time, he knew that he was only a layman when it came to understanding the highly complex laws that governed the workings of the universe. Nevertheless, he had grasped the notion that space-time is not a fixture, but can be distorted. Time can be speeded up or slowed down, depending on how quickly a person is travelling—or at least Einstein had said something like this. Maybe he had rapidly aged as Melchizedek but, in the life he had left before being transferred back to this earlier incarnation, barely a day had gone by. If this were the case, than perhaps he had not yet been missed.

His thoughts now turned to the present, and the fabled Garden of Eden into which he had now been deposited. The Hebrew Scriptures state that this was where Adam and Eve lived, but Mel had always thought of this story as allegorical—symbolic of how humankind had at first been given everything, but had then squandered it by yielding to temptation. Maybe the fact that the eyes of this first human couple were then opened to see the harsh realities of life was not a bad thing, he had mused. Yes, this may have been the cradle of civilization, at least according to the creationist account, but he would not waste time searching for evidence that Adam had once lived here. [9]

Whilst he was eager to explore the countryside around him, Mel's first action would have to be finding something to eat. There would be no difficulty in drinking because, as Michael had promised, he was already near to a stream that provided a ready supply of life-giving water.

He had seen how many artists had used their creative skills to try and illustrate what the Garden of Eden may have looked like. These paintings usually depicted a bucolic, pastoral scene with verdant meadows, lush trees, cuddly animals romping in the fields, and colorful birds inhabiting the skies. The trees are always shown as being either covered with blossom or laden with fruit. In the distance, misty mountain-tops stand proudly under fluffy white clouds. Flowers of every hue deck the hillsides and, of course, the sun is always shining. The overall impression given is invariably one of idyllic peace and harmony.

Looking around him, Mel could see that the "Garden" was indeed an oasis, and a very fertile one at that. But it was not quite as depicted by the artists, most of whom would have inhabited the western world and, therefore, have painted halcyon landscapes in keeping with their western ideals. Yes, he could see a variety of trees and shrubs, many of which bore fruit. Some of the tall palms had coconuts growing under their canopies of green fronds, whilst others were varieties that produced dates that appeared to be ripe for harvesting. Rather more accessible were the trees laden with pomegranates, peaches or olives and yes, as might be expected in this fabled garden, there were also fig trees! To complete this arboreal collection, Mel could see walnuts growing on nearby branches.

If these trees continued to bear fruit for the whole time I am here, then I shall not starve, Mel said to himself. To satiate his immediate hunger, he plucked some of the fruits and sat down to enjoy a welcome breakfast. He then went down to the stream to drink some water from his cupped hands, and was delighted to see small fish swimming beneath the surface, nibbling green algae from the rocks. Here was a chance to have a change of diet, he thought; maybe there are other foodstuffs in this haven to further supplement the menu.

Now refreshed and eager to explore further afield, Mel slid the knife—his only possession—into the belt of his tunic, and set off at a brisk pace. He decided to follow a path that led upstream to where he thought the central pool of the oasis would be. Should he not succeed in finding a more suitable place to establish a camp that would be his home for the next year, at least he would be able to trace his way back to where he had started from.

His mind recalled Daniel Defoe's story of Robinson Crusoe, who was no doubt inspired by the real-life experiences of Alexander Selkirk during the four years that he spent marooned on a Pacific island. Crusoe had certainly used a lot of initiative to make his life comfortable, and Mel hoped that he could remember some of these activities in order to make his own stay more tolerable. There was one important difference, however. Whilst Crusoe acquired a companion—Man Friday—Mel was on his own. Again, his thoughts turned to Angelina. If only she were by his side now, he would not worry even if he could never leave this sanctuary.

What a fertile place it was, and how colorful, he mused. Whilst Mel was unable to identify all the varieties of flowers that clothed the banks of the stream and surrounded the trees, he could see that many of the artists had been accurate in reflecting at least this aspect of the Garden. He soon became aware of the familiar sound of bees going about their business, collecting nectar from nature's floral display. Bees? If there are bees, then there must be bees' nests. If there are nests, then there must be honey. If he could find some of this, then it would be yet another welcome item to supplement his diet.

As he continued his walk, Mel wondered what animal life there might be here, in addition to the fish and the insects. Hopefully, this will not include the serpent that tempted Eve! Looking up, he noticed colorful birds flying high in the air and occasionally calling to each other. There might be eggs I can collect, he thought, but it would mean climbing up trees to search for them, and they would probably be very small. Eventually he arrived at the edge of the pool responsible for providing the water that gave life to this oasis. As it trickled out in several small streams that irrigated the land beyond, it was constantly being replenished by an underground flow that originated from where the rains fell, many miles away.

And there, swimming on this precious reservoir, were birds that resembled the ducks he had seen many times on the village ponds near the home from which he had been transported. Where there are ducks, there must be nests, and where there are nests then there will be eggs—and of a size that would provide a useful meal. Mel had no hesitation in deciding that he would not kill and eat any of the birds themselves. He had always avoided meat when there was an adequate alternative available, and there was no need to change this habit now. Not only that, but he would collect eggs only when he knew they had been freshly laid, so that no embryo would have had the time to develop.

Already, in just one morning, he had found a range of fruits and nuts, fish in the streams, and the likelihood of honey once he had searched for it. Now there were eggs, and he had yet to see if he could find any edible roots or green plants that would fulfill his need for vegetables.

Yes, he would have a balanced diet to serve him well during this enforced exile. However, it would be a bonus if he were able to cook some of this food. Firstly he would need to be able to make a fire; boy scouts had been taught how to do this, and Mel was keen to give it a try. He collected some small dried twigs from under the trees, along with some of the thicker branches that were lying, broken on the ground. Using his precious knife, he selected a strong stick from this pile, and sharpened one end of it. Searching around in the undergrowth, he found a larger piece of dried branch, and used the point of his knife to create a small hollow near one side of it. Finally, he cut a v-shaped slot next to this recess.

Mel was now ready to start his experiment. Placing some dried moss near the slot, he inserted the pointed stick into the hollow and, using the palms of his hands, twisted it backwards and forwards as rapidly as possible. He continued until exhaustion made him pause. No sign of any flame yet. He touched the wood with a finger, but withdrew it rapidly; the wood was hot! Encouraged, he recommenced his efforts. Soon he was rewarded. First a little smoke, then a burning smell from the moss, and then—a flame. Quickly, Mel placed the smaller twigs over the little fire, and then the larger branches. It only took another minute or two for the kindling to alight. Life was getting better and better!

Satisfied with his discoveries and achievements on this, his first day, Mel decided he would make his permanent base here, under the trees next to the oasis. Provided the weather remained warm and dry, as it was at the present, he would not need much in the way of shelter; he could always retreat under the canopy of leaves behind him if there should be an unexpected rain shower. There was little preparation to do, apart from choosing some level ground and covering it with layers of long grass in order to provide a mattress on which he could sleep. Now that had mastered the art of making fire, he would collect a quantity of fallen branches and keep them nearby as a fuel supply.

Mel's thoughts now turned to seeing if he could make containers that would hold water, and maybe even allow him to heat some of his food on the fire. He decided that first he would use his knife to try and hollow out the centre of a piece cut from one of the larger branches, to form a wooden cup. His first attempt was crude, but it did enable him to scoop up some water and drink from it. Secondly, he would search the banks of the pool to see if he could find some clay. This he would use to attempt to make a pot by building up rings around a circular base. When it was dry, he could try to harden it in a pit filled with burning wood.

All this handiwork would require trial and error, but he had plenty of time; it would keep him busy and stop him thinking of all the things that he missed. He could see that the sun was nearing the western horizon, and decided that he had done enough on this, his first day. Now he must gather some more fruit for his evening meal, along with a few of the walnuts he had seen earlier. Tomorrow he would explore further, and try to find different edibles to provide him with a more varied menu to enjoy.

———————

Over the coming days and weeks, Mel's skill in fashioning what he needed from the available materials increased significantly. He soon had a small selection of wooden containers, and was especially pleased with a fork and spoon that he had carved from tree branches. His attempts to make clay cooking pots were rather less successful, because the lack of a sufficiently high temperature in his fire pit resulted in vessels that were still slightly porous. However, when he tried shaping some clay around half a coconut shell, removing it for the firing, and then refitting it, he was delighted to find that this hybrid pot was watertight and could be used for cooking.

Pleased that he could now add boiled vegetables or stews to his fare, Mel searched for additional foodstuffs and found a chard-like leafy plant, dandelions and some nettles. By chance, he had noticed what appeared to be tubers partly exposed in the soil. When he had dug down a little, he was able to harvest what he was sure was a form of sweet potato. In addition, he had discovered a primitive form of barley growing wild in the meadows. When the grains, leaves and roots were added to his cooking pot, they made a nourishing meal, especially if accompanied by a couple of poached duck eggs.

Mel was quite pleased with his construction of a simple fish trap. He had collected some thin, flexible branches, and twisted them together to form a funnel, open at one end. When strategically placed in the stream so that the water flowed into the opening, he did not have to wait long before some of the fish entered the trap and found their exit blocked. He had released the smaller ones back into the water, and only saved those large enough for a meal. These, roasted over the open fire, with sweet potatoes baked in the embers, was a main course to which he could look forward. To complete the banquet, he usually enjoyed a desert of fruits plucked from the trees, or piece of honeycomb stolen from the bees' nest.

When he was not fabricating utensils, or gathering food, Mel wasted no opportunity to explore the extent of the Garden. It was much larger than he had previously imagined. He had managed to reach the foothills of the distant mountains, but had resisted the temptation to spend the night there so that he could climb to the top the next day. There were still some unknowns here, and he preferred to return to the security of his simple base camp and few possessions each day at nightfall.

Although the artists had been fairly accurate in depicting a peaceful landscape, clothed in green and embellished with flowers of every color, they had been wrong in one aspect. There were no animals romping in the fields, or mammals of any kind so far as Mel could tell; the wildlife comprised only birds, fish, and insects. He was mindful of the biblical tale of Eve's temptation by the serpent, and had kept a wary eye open for snakes, but was thankful that none had revealed themselves to him—yet! Being close in latitude to the equator, neither the temperature nor daylight hours changed much during his time in the Garden.

Indeed, it was a pleasant place in which to be exiled and, as had been promised, all that he needed was available, provided he made the effort to find it. He just wished he had a companion, and especially Angelina. Mel realized that he was continuing to grow older at a faster rate than would be expected from the passing weeks and months. He estimated that he had now reached the age of about thirty years, the same as he was in the life from which he had been so rudely transported.

There was just one other thing that was starting to worry him. His earthly father, Nir, had told him that sometimes the sign of the priesthood included horns and a tail. Mel had only been reborn with the serpent scales on his chest. He had kept feeling his body to check that the other manifestations were not there, but now he was sure he could detect small lumps just where horns and a tail would be. So far, they were not too prominent and could be kept concealed. But what if they started to grow?

Chapter 5

SALEM

The first thing that Mel saw when he opened his eyes after a refreshing night's sleep was Archangel Michael standing in front of him. "It is time to depart, Melchizedek," he said.

Mel was still only half awake, and all he could think of to say was, "Has a full year passed already?"

"Yes, it is time for your mission to begin," Michael confirmed.

"Are Nir and the rest of the family safe?"

"Yes. The rains beat down mercilessly for forty days and nights, and the ark was soon afloat. The water continued to rise for another hundred days. Eventually the vessel came to rest on Mount Ararat, but it was more than two hundred days later before the land was dry enough for them, and the animals, to disembark."

Mel was relieved to hear this, but he wanted to know more about what had happened outside of the calm haven that had been his home during this time of destruction elsewhere.

"All life in this part of the world perished in the flood, as punishment for being disobedient to the Lord, but the more distant countries did not suffer the same fate."

"I shall be sorry to leave this peaceful garden," said Mel. "Shall I ever be able to return?"

"Unfortunately not," replied Michael. "On our journey here you were surprised that this region was dry land. In a little while, the rising sea level will burst over the land bridge that protects this valley, and the garden will disappear beneath the waters for ever."

Mel was sad to learn that this oasis paradise would soon be no more, but was glad that he had been privileged to spend the past year here, before it was lost. At least the birds and insects will be able to fly away and find some other sanctuary, he mused.

"Where are you taking me?," he asked his companion.

"To the land of Canaan, which has escaped the flood.[10] The city of Salem is over a thousand kilometers north-west of here. No one must see how you were transported there, so I shall not take you inside the entrance gate. Instead I shall leave you some way off, near the main road to the city. You will have to complete the remainder of the journey on your own."

"Is there a particular reason for this?," Mel queried.

"The inhabitants of Salem, along with the rest of Canaan, have long been expecting the arrival of a great leader and High Priest. They will recognize that you are that person, because you have the Badge of Priesthood on your breast."

Mel had no wish to be reminded of the serpent scales that covered much of his chest but, before he had the chance to frame his next question, Michael spoke again. "You will need to plan your entry through the city gates so that it is befitting of the office you will hold. One of the farmers will lend you an animal on which to ride, and the people will give you an enthusiastic welcome when they see you coming.[11] Once inside the walls, you will continue your journey until you reach the king's residence, which is where you will live."

Anticipating what Mel was just about to ask, the Archangel said, "You will receive guidance from El Elyon, the same Lord who guides me. If you need help, then make your wishes known to him in your prayers." Curtailing the opportunity for any further questions, the archangel announced, "It is time to go now."

It would serve no purpose to try and delay the departure, so Mel made sure his precious knife was firmly secured in his belt.

Leaving all his other possessions behind, he climbed astride Michael's back and they ascended into the air. As was the case when he had been transported to the Garden, this journey could have been completed in an instant, but Mel asked if he could have some views of the land beneath them.

The green oasis, with its sparkling pool and trickling streams gradually receded. They firstly passed over the remaining part of the dry valley, before coming to the vast expanse of land that had been flooded. At one point, the Archangel pointed downwards and said, "Here is where you lived with Noah and his family, and where the ark was built." Mel could see nothing of the house or any other signs of habitation—sadly, the flood had washed them all away.

Eventually they reached the end of the area of devastation, and were soaring over the fertile crescent of Canaan. After searching for a suitable place to land, they descended to a field out of sight of any of the local inhabitants. "I repeat that nobody must see you arrive, or know from where you have come," said Michael. Mel looked around him. They must now be in a valley, because the land to the north was a gradual incline leading up to an elevated plateau. There, on the distant horizon, he could just make out the outlines of a city, which his companion confirmed was indeed Salem, his future home.

"I shall leave you now," said Michael. "Remember, enter the city in a manner that befits a King and High Priest, and carry out your duties with wisdom and compassion."

"Will you be visiting me again?," asked Mel, still feeling overwhelmed by the responsibilities that awaited him.

"I do not know," was the reply. "But I shall be aware of your progress, and will carry out whatever El Elyon asks me to do." With that, the Archangel departed and once again Mel was alone. He sat down on a stone wall at the edge of the field, to try and gather his thoughts before doing anything else. It did not take long for him to realize that, at this stage, he had little alternative but to start to make his way toward the city, and then let fate take its course.

Leaving the field, Mel soon came to the dusty road that would lead to his destination, and started the long walk up the gently-sloping hill. By mid-day he was both tired and thirsty. Seeing a farmhouse close by, he approached it and knocked on the door. When the farmer emerged, Mel asked him if he could please have a drink of water from the well. The farmer agreed, and was about to fetch a cup when he noticed Mel's bare chest, visible through the gap left open in his tunic to help him keep cool in the heat of the day.

"You have the Badge of Priesthood on your breast," the farmer shrieked, "You are the one for whom we have waited for such a long time." He then fell to his knees, in humble submission. Feeling rather embarrassed, but also thinking that he would probably have to become used to such adulation, Mel bade the man stand. Now somewhat calmer, the farmer said, "Sir, I am your servant Benjamin; we do not have much to offer, but it would be an honor if you would share a table with my wife, Sarah, and me, and receive refreshment before you continue your journey."

Mel was grateful to accept the farmer's kind invitation, and was pleased to go into the house to escape from the heat of the sun. This would be a chance for him to try and learn something about the situation in this part of the world, before he was thrust into the position of leadership. The meal was simple but sustaining: freshly baked bread, cheese made by Sarah from milk produced by the farmer's own animals, and a little wine.

Wondering how to ask questions for which somebody of his status should already have the answers, he said with as much authority as he could muster, "I am Mel . . . Melchizedek. I have been sent by El Elyon to be King and High Priest of Salem." He had nearly fallen into the trap of referring to himself by his modern name, and resolved to try and remember to always use his priestly epithet. "You say that my arrival had been anticipated. What do the people expect of me?"

"We have had priests before you to give us spiritual guidance, including Methusalem, Enoch, Aleem, and Arusan," Benjamin replied. "And we have also had a succession of local chieftains to protect us. But now we have neither." [12]

"What happened to them?"

"The last priest was childless, and therefore left no successor when he died. Our chieftain became ambitious, and thought he could conquer the land east of the River Jordan. He never returned."

"So Salem is now like a ship without a captain," Mel commented.

"Yes Sir. The people have become lawless, and have started to worship idols. We have already suffered raiding parties from neighboring tribes, and we fear a major invasion.[13] Those of us who remain loyal to El Elyon have prayed for a savior, and now our prayers have been answered."

At least Mel was now a little clearer on what his role would be, although he still felt himself very unprepared and inadequate. It was important not to show this, he reasoned, but to display an air of authority and confidence at all times. Michael had promised more than once that he would receive all the guidance he needed, and he must trust him in this. The sooner he made a start on his mission, the better, he reasoned.

"Thank you for this information, Benjamin, and for your generous hospitality," he said. If the people are expecting me, I must delay no longer as there is still some way to go before nightfall."

"But you must not make the journey on foot," the farmer replied. "I shall lend you my most sturdy donkey. It has been fed and watered, and will take you to the city. Leave the animal in the Palace stables, and I shall come and collect it later."

Mel expressed his grateful thanks to Benjamin for his kindness, and to his wife Sarah. He did not have any money to give him in return, so the only reward he could offer was to say, "I shall remember how much you have helped me, Benjamin. If you encounter any difficulties once I am established, please come and ask for my help." With that, he sat astride the donkey and continued on his way to the city on the hill.

Fortified by their respective refreshments, man and animal made good progress. The road passed by the Spring of En-rogel, where women were filling their water jars with the life-sustaining liquid. It was still afternoon when they were close enough to

Salem for Mel to see that the gates in the south wall were closed. There were other travelers on the road now, and he was conscious of receiving a few furtive glances, as well as some more pointed staring. This was sometimes followed by excited babble amongst the people. Was it his imagination, or were their numbers steadily growing as he approached the gates?

Before Mel needed to worry about how he was going to enter the city, the gates were opened wide before him. It was clear that there was now a crowd of people lining both sides of the road, and some were waving homemade flags of colored cloth tied to sticks. He could even hear sounds of cheering, and shouts of welcome. Trying to fulfill his resolve to remain authoritative and confident, he sat upright on the donkey as he rode, but could not resist occasionally returning the waves.

The road, which was now paved with stone, led through the gates and continued northwards through the city. The donkey seemed to know which way to go without any guidance, so Mel let it continue whilst he looked around at the urban landscape. Although he had entered through gates, he now noticed that the wall did not extend right around the city. Already he had the first idea of how he could demonstrate his leadership—he would organize the completion of the wall, and thus help the people to defend themselves against the invaders that the farmer had mentioned.

To his left he saw adults with their children splashing around in a pool, and filling their water jars from a steam that ran into it through a tunnel. Recalling the Bible stories of old, he surmised that this must be the Pool of Siloam where, many years in the future, Jesus would heal a blind man. Narrow streets crisscrossed the road and, on both sides, there was a maze of alleyways crammed with little dwellings.

Although situated at an important crossing point of the main north-south trade route, and the highway that ran west-east from the Mediteranian to the lands beyond the river Jordan, the city that would become the future Jerusalem was still small—less than one hundred and fifty meters wide, and only eight hundred meters long.

Mel need not have been concerned about finding his way to the Palace, because the crowd had obviously anticipated his destination. The excited bystanders stopped at the gateway to an imposing building that would become his home. Further along the road to the north he could see what appeared to be the Temple, where he would be expected to provide spiritual leadership, and perform the rituals of the priesthood. [14]

Once inside the little courtyard, several men and women came out of the house and bowed down before him. He surmised that these must be the ones who had served the previous leaders. Mel alighted from the faithful animal that had brought him to this place, and one of the men led it round the back of the building to the stables. He made his way to the door of the residence, which was being held open by one of the servants. Before entering, he turned and gave a final dignified wave to the people at the gates. As he went in to the Palace, once again different thoughts and emotions competed for dominance in his mind. Yes, he would no doubt be comfortable living here, but his mission was about to begin. It was already clear that much was expected of him. Would he be able to succeed, he wondered?

Chapter 6

CONFUSION

Once inside the building, Mel was approached by a man who seemed to have an air of authority about him. "Lord Melchizedek," he said, "I am Obadiah, the Chief Servant. I welcome you on behalf of the palace staff. We have heard that you are the special one, with the Badge of Priesthood on your breast, and we have been looking forward to your coming."

Thank you Obadiah," Mel replied. "There is much to do, and I need the loyal support of everyone here if I am to succeed."

"I promise to serve you to the best of my ability. What do you wish me to do?"

Mel was in no position to issue specific instructions at this time, as he first needed to be appraised of the needs of this community. He thus responded to Obadiah's question: "It has been a tiring journey for me, and we shall be able discuss this over the days to come. As for today, it is already late. Can you please arrange for some food and give me a brief tour of the palace."

Whilst the meal was being prepared, Obadiah gave Mel a guided tour of the building. Despite its palatial epithet and outward appearance, inside it was comparatively modest in design. The largest room on the ground floor was the throne room where the King received visitors, held court, and gave banquets for important dignitaries. There was a smaller room for private dining and study, areas for food storage and preparation, plus accommodation for the servants. Upstairs was the king's bedchamber, along with several rooms for guests.

After his extended holiday in the Garden of Eden—for in retrospect that was the only way to describe it—it had been a very eventful day. Mel was glad to accept the meal of vegetable and lentil stew, cheese, and bread, accompanied by a goblet of excellent wine, that the servants had prepared for him, and then retire to his chambers. Although he needed a quiet place to think about how he would try to cope with the awesome responsibilities thrust upon him, the chance to sleep in a proper bed for the first time in a year was beckoning. Once he had lain down on the mattress, his weariness did not permit more than a moment of contemplation before sleep overtook him.

But the dreams soon came—or were they dreams? He was back in the high street where he and Angelina had been window-shopping for furniture. His fiancée had gone on ahead of him, and he had lost sight of her. Oh, how he missed her. Where was she now? Despite his leaden feet, Mel tried to quicken his pace. Was that Angelina he could see in the distance? Whomever it was soon disappeared, but he continued struggling to reach the spot where he had last seen the figure, glancing hopefully through shop windows as he tried to hurry along. And there she was, seated in the hairdresser's salon in front of a wash basin, just about to lean over and have her hair shampooed.

It caused some consternation when Mel rushed into the shop and went straight to Angelina. "I lost you," he blurted out almost hysterically. "Why did you rush off like that?"

"But I told you I was already late for the hairdresser's appointment," she said. "You were so preoccupied, looking at that lounge suite we could not afford, that you obviously did not listen to what I was saying. Typical man!"

Others in the salon must have heard this last comment, as the sound of giggling was quite evident. Mel now felt rather foolish, and tried to excuse himself. "Sorry," I forgot," he mumbled. "How long will you be?"

"Let's meet up at the coffee shop at noon; we can have a sand-wich there, and then look at some more furniture this afternoon."

And with that, Mel sidled out of the salon, trying his best to appear nonchalant, much to the relief—but also amusement—of the other women who were there. He needed time to collect his thoughts, so he made his way to the coffee shop, ordered a hot drink, and sat down near the window. What was happening to him? he wondered. How had he not understood Angelina's simple statement about where she was going? He now started to feel slightly dizzy, and his vision began to blur. With an effort, he man-aged to regain his concentration, but this attack had just added to his concern.

Mel took a drink from his coffee cup, hoping that it would sharpen his alertness. However, he found himself drifting into daydreams again. It was as if his mind was trying to lead him else-where, to images of some place far away. There was an air of famil-iarity about it all, but he could not as yet come up with a name. He had to keep digging his nails into the palms of his hands to try and help him stay awake, and in the present. But this was not always successful.

"A penny for your thoughts, Mel?" It was Angelina, back al-ready from the hairdressers.

"My, but you have been quick," he said with a start. "I thought you said that you would only be finished at noon."

"It is now ten minutes after twelve," she replied. "When I came in you seemed to be deep in thought, and I was not even sure that you were awake."

Mel had to come up with an answer that would convince Angelina that he was not completely mad. "I was just thinking of that three-piece suite that I had my eye on this morning, but now I think it might look out of place in the lounge at Salem."

His fiancé was puzzled. "Salem . . . . . Salem. Where is that, and what does it have to do with the house we are hoping to buy when we are married?"

Oh dear, now I have completely messed things up, Mel thought, thankfully having now regained full wakefulness. He better think of something quickly. On impulse he said, "Ah! This is just what I think we should call our own house, when we have one."

"Not sure that I like it, it sounds foreign," Angeline commented. "Where did you get this name from?"

Mel realized that this was the place he had been struggling to remember, the images of which had invaded his mind a few moments ago. He did not have time to try and analyze why, but had to continue with this theme now that he had started it. "This is an ancient name for Jerusalem," he explained.

"But we are not particularly religious, so why suggest a name so strongly associated with such beliefs, not to mention one with a long history of conflict because the different faiths there cannot live together in harmony?"

"Yes, I agree that there are often sectarian troubles in that part of the world, but the name of that city has a meaning that I thought would suit our future love-nest."

Angelina's tone of voice suggested that she was still very skeptical of the idea. "Alright, tell me then," she said. "But it better be convincing."

"It means 'peace', 'perfect peace'," Mel replied.

Her expression visibly softened. "Oh, it's so sweet of you to think of that," she said. "We can keep this in mind, but let's not make a final decision right now. When we find our dream house, some other name might be more suitable."

Mel was glad to have wriggled out of the hole that he had inadvertently dug for himself, but he still could not understand why both the images and the name had entered his mind uninvited.

Angelina was speaking again. "Are you sure you are feeling alright, Mel? You seemed very vague when I came in, and it looked like it took you some time to remember where you were."

"Sorry, love, it is just that I have not been sleeping too well lately."

She reached out and gently took Mel's hand. "Tell me truthfully, are you having doubts about us getting married? If you are, you must be honest with me."

"Good heavens no, Angelina," he replied. "The day we get married and I can call you my wife, will be the happiest one of my life."

"Then what is troubling you so much that you cannot sleep?"

"I don't know, but I am having many dreams of places far away." Trying to reassure both his fiancée as well as himself, Mel added: "Maybe these represent possible honeymoon destinations."

This seemed to satisfy Angelina, at least for the present, so they collected their lunch from the counter and changed the conversation to more routine topics.

The trawl round the shops continued after lunch. Mel tried his best to act normally and say the right things but, deep in his mind, he was still struggling to try and understand why his thoughts kept pulling him toward a different time and place. Was he literally going insane—perhaps developing a schizophrenic, duel personality? If this were the case, it would not be fair to keep it from Angelina, and he would have to seek specialist medical help. On the other hand, he may be just worrying unduly, what with the various pressures he was under regarding both his work and private life. Perhaps this was taking a greater toll on his coping resources than he realized.

He needed time by himself to thoroughly think through his situation and what he should do about it. It was, however, important that he should not give Angelina the impression that he was losing interest in her, or the wedding; she had already put such a question to him earlier. After the shopping excursion, and an evening dinner together, Mel confessed that the stress he was under was affecting him, and that it would be a good idea if he retired to bed early to try and recover. Next day would be a Sunday, so they could enjoy a time of leisure together and, hopefully, he would be better company. Angelina understood, although she was still hiding some concerns, having seen for herself how vague and confused Mel had been earlier.

Once back in his bachelor flat, Mel poured himself a generous measure of whiskey as a nightcap, hoping that this would help him to settle down and sleep. He propped himself up in bed and, sipping his drink, reviewed the events of the day. It had started off normally, with meeting Angelina and looking in the furniture shops. Then he had lost her, even though he had apparently been told that she was going to hurry ahead to the hairdressers. Why did he not remember where she had gone? And why did he seem semi paralyzed when trying to follow her?

Then, when sitting by himself in the coffee shop, why did he start to feel dizzy and have mental images of a distant place that he could not immediately recognize? Even more surprisingly, why did he blurt out the name 'Salem', and how did he know what it meant? Finally, why was time playing tricks on him? On the one hand, he appeared to be moving in slow motion when he had tried to catch Angelina up, but then the time waiting for her in the coffee shop had flashed by in an instant.

Once again, the thought of impending madness invaded his mind, but he tried to brush this aside—at least for the moment. There must be an alternative explanation, no matter how improbable it might be. Could he be experiencing memories of a past life, he wondered? Whilst not being a strong believer in the idea of reincarnation, Mel did not want to completely rule out this possibility. Stories he had heard from other people had failed to convince him, but was he now undergoing this for himself? Were the words and images he kept experiencing evidence of what could be a previous existence?

Whilst this idea brought little comfort to Mel, it was at least something he could try and investigate by finding out whatever he could about the places and times that were intruding, uninvited, into his mind. However, doubtful as it seemed that this idea of a past life could be true, if a person could be born as a different individual, would he or she then still have detailed memories of their earlier situation? [15]

It would be remarkable, he mused, if sufficient elements could indeed be recalled to construct a meaningful account of that different time and place. Maybe this could then help to explain historical events for which there remain unanswered questions. But then who would believe a person alive today who claimed to have been present when the Romans invaded Britain, or who had witnessed that assignation of President Lincoln?

Mel tried to give further consideration to this notion, and the research he would now carry out on the images that had been invading his thoughts. But this was not the time, as his alcoholic nightcap was now exerting its influence. His eyes closed, and he quickly succumbed to the sedative effects of the amber nectar that is one of Scotland's finest exports.

Chapter 7

THE KING

"Lord Melchizedek, Sir, it is time to wake up." The voice was deferential, whilst conveying a sense of both firmness and urgency. Mel stirred, wondering in his semi-conscious state why someone was disturbing his sleep by talking to somebody else, and hoping that whomever it was would go away.

But here it went again. "Sir, it is long past daybreak, and people have been asking to see you." Mel reluctantly opened his eyes and saw two of the palace servants standing next to his bed. It was indeed daylight, and the early morning sun was streaming through the window, now unhindered by the curtain that must have been opened by those who were attending him. The realization that he was back in Salem took a moment to register in his not yet fully alert brain. Meeting Angelina again must have just been a dream—or was what he was experiencing now a dream? He had no opportunity to think further about this now, but must try and cope with the immediate situation.

"You say that people have been asking to see me. Who are they, and what do they want?" Mel asked the servants.

One of the men replied: "Sir, the twelve Elders of Salem came early to request an audience with you. They have long awaited your coming, and wish to explain to you the difficulties and challenges facing this city, and to find out what you will do to help them."

Mel was aware that he had been sent to Salem to fulfill two roles, one being the King and the other the High Priest. He was not sure how he could combine these, but decided that it would be safer to deal with them one at a time. Obviously he now had to take on the role of King, and try to cope with the tasks of leadership.

"I shall meet with them," Mel responded with his best authoritative voice. "Please invite them to come at noon and meet me in the throne room. We can offer them some hospitality whilst we talk."

"Very good Sir, we shall inform the leaders of your invitation, and prepare some bread and broth to eat." With that, the servants departed, leaving Mel to gather his thoughts and decide what to do next.

He noticed that the sun was still barely half way to its zenith, so he estimated there were nearly three hours before his meeting with the deputation of Elders. Perhaps there was a sundial or shadow clock somewhere in the building that would provide a more accurate measure of time. He would investigate this later. In the meantime, Mel decided that his first priority would be to become more familiar with the Palace that would be his residence for some time to come, starting with his royal bedchamber.

There was a bowl of fruit, olives, and nuts on a table at the foot of the bed, and he snacked on these in lieu of the sort of breakfast he was used to eating. The servants had not mentioned breakfast being ready, so he assumed he was expected to avail himself of what had been left here for him. He was to learn that this was the normal practice in this part of the world at that time, and that the first proper meal of the day was taken about noon, with the main feast being in the evening when the work was done. [16]

The next consideration was the mundane but necessary provision for ablutions. Mel realized that he would have to become used to the primitive pit latrines that would be found outside the building, with just portable receptacles being available indoors. But then what about washing? He had seen people bathing in the

Pool of Siloam when he arrived at Salem yesterday, but he would have to see if a similar provision was also available in the Palace grounds. In the meantime, an amphora of water had been left for him in the room, along with an earthenware basin.

Mel could not resist smiling to himself when he compared the facilities in this room with the wash bowls, jugs and chamber pots that were still being provided in some holiday boarding houses to which he had been taken as a youngster. Progress had indeed been slow! What did surprise him was that there was a block of something that looked remarkably like soap. Although apparently this was meant to be used mainly for washing wool and other textiles, he would be happy to follow the practice learned in his parallel existence and use it on himself. [17]

He now turned his attention to clothing, and discovered that a variety of items was available to him. Thankfully this included some basic undergarments, along with a range of long gowns and cloaks. These were mostly dyed with dark colors, with some being embroidered with gold thread. One flowing terracotta-colored robe was presumably for formal occasions, and he decided he should wear this for his meeting later in the morning. He would complete this outfit with a black and gold helmet-shaped head covering. In addition to all this rather cumbersome apparel, Mel was pleased to see that there were some more casual clothing items that could be worn on non-formal occasions, including a hip-length jerkin and breeches. [18]

Having explored all he could in his bedchamber, Mel washed himself, dressed in a manner that befitted his kingly status, and went downstairs to prepare for his meeting with the group of Elders. Before they arrived, however, he wished to find out more about how the Palace was organized. Seeking out Obadiah, the Chief Servant, he took him into the small side room, invited him to sit down, and started to ask him questions.

"How long have you been in service at the palace?" Mel asked the bearded, middle-aged man sitting opposite him.

"Lord Melchizedek, I have worked here since I was a young boy. My first position was as a stable-hand. I labored hard, and was then given more important work to do. When the previous incumbent died, the last chieftain promoted me to my present role, before he left to fight his own war."

"I am sure you justified your appointment," Mel commented. "How many servants work here?"

"Sir, we are not great in number. The Chancellor, Jacob, and Secretary, Daniel, report directly to you, as do I. In my role I am responsible for supervising the Butler and his serving staff, the Head Cook and the kitchen workers, the Housekeeper and her chambermaids, the stable-hands, and the Palace guards. We are no more than thirty people. I regret that no concubines live in the Palace but, if it is your wish, I can arrange some for you."

Mel was somewhat taken-aback by this final comment, and was quick to assure his Chief Servant that he doubted this would be necessary. "Thank you, Obadiah, I am confident that you are all loyal and perform your duties excellently. Would you please now send Chancellor Jacob to me." With that, Obadiah withdrew and, after a moment or two, Jacob entered the room.

The Chancellor appeared to be older than the Chief Servant, grey haired and with a long white beard. He wore a black cloak, and a pointed hat in the same color but with the addition of some white fur around the rim. The man seemed to be a little nervous, but bowed respectfully toward Mel and said, "My Lord Melchizedek, I am at your service, what instructions do you have for me?"

Mel did his best to but Jacob at his ease. "Please sit down so we can talk in comfort. Before I am in a position to give any instructions, I need to know what the current situation is concerning the palace finances. How do we obtain the income to run this place, and is it sufficient?"

"Sir, the citizens of Salem do their best to pay their tithes and taxes to support both the Palace and the Temple, but many of them are poor. Marauding nomads often come and rob the farmers and artisans who live outside of the city gates. Because we are not fully protected by a wall, the invaders are also bold enough to make raids into Salem itself."

"Are we not in a position to protect our city and our people?" Mel asked.

"The chieftains we have had up to now have tried, but our last one was more interested in conquering other lands to get rich, than in caring for the local population. He made me give him all the money that was left in the treasury, to pay the fighting men who went with him on his last escapade. We do benefit from Salem being situated on both north-south and west-east trading routes, and a little money trickles in from travelers who pass through here and purchase supplies. However, many of the peasants have difficulty in paying their dues, and some of the palace staff have not received their full wages for a long time."

The Chancellor seemed weary and weighed down with his troubles, so Mel made an effort to reassure him. "I am sure you have tried your best, and I am grateful for your loyalty and that of those who work here, despite them not being adequately paid. The Elders will be arriving shortly. I shall hear what they have to say, and we will work hard to formulate a plan to protect the city and bring peace and prosperity to this land." These words appeared to visibly raise Jacob's spirits, and he left the room, leaving Mel to consider what he had been told by these two senior members of the royal household. Urgent action was certainly needed, but did he have the ability to meet the challenge?

After what only seemed to be a few minutes, one of the servants came into the room to inform him that the Elders were starting to arrive, and that the meal would soon be served. Still trying to think through possible options open to him, he made his entrance into the large throne room. The twelve Elders immediately knelt down in humble submission. Mel still remained inwardly embarrassed by all this deference, when he still thought of himself as just an ordinary person thrust into a situation not of his choosing. However, the people clearly acknowledged him as their leader and savior, and he had little alternative but to play this role to the best of his ability.

"Please rise," he said. "The food is just about to be served, so make yourselves comfortable on the couches and let us refresh ourselves before discussing matters of state."

One of the men spoke up. "Lord Melchizedek, I am Sirach, and my role is Foreman of the City Elders. We thank you for agreeing to meet us so soon after your arrival, and for offering us your hospitality. We shall do as you say, and enjoy this meal before raising our concerns." With that, the serving staff brought the simple fare of a broth fortified with crushed and roasted grain, accompanied by freshly baked bread. Bowls containing a variety of fruits were also placed before the diners.

Once the meal was over and the servants had cleared the tables, Mel invited Sirach to state why the Elders had needed to see him so urgently. The Foreman stood up and said, "Sir, the citizens of Salem have worked hard and remained loyal to the previous chieftains. We have tried to pay our taxes and tithes, but we have not been protected from the invaders that often come and steal our crops, the goods that we produce, and our money."

"Yes, I have already been informed of this by my Chancellor," replied Mel. "What do you know about these invaders?"

"Those we have identified are Amorites who come from the semi-arid regions on the fringes of the Syrian Desert. They live a nomadic existence, so do not stay in the same area for long. This makes it difficult for us to track them down when we try to retaliate."

"Do you have any specific ideas on what should be done?," Mel asked.

"We have discussed this among ourselves," Sirach said. "The city wall is not yet complete because there is no money available to pay the builders. If a way can be found to finish it, then at least those within Salem will be protected."

"I agree with you, and I promise that the wall will be completed," Mel responded.

The Foreman continued: "Thank you Sir, but many people also live in their own farms and homesteads away from the main city, so they will still remain vulnerable to attack."

"It appears that we also need troops or guards to patrol the whole of our territory both day and night," commented Mel.

"Indeed this would likely solve the problem, and we have suggested this to previous leaders, but they told us once again that they had no money to pay for such a police force." With that final comment, Sirach resumed his seat.

Mel addressed they assembled group, "I have heard your complaints and your suggestions. Is there anything else you wish to say to me at this time?" Nobody offered to raise additional issues, so he continued, "It seems to me that the main factor holding up action is the lack of funding." He paused, and noted respectful nods of agreement from those present. "The best means of raising money is by exporting goods. What do we have in Canaan that people in neighboring countries would want to buy?"

Another of the Elders stood up. "Lord Melchizedek, my name is Jonathan, and I employ men to help me extract the purple dye, murex, from sea snails that we harvest from the Mediteranian Sea. This is in great demand, and fetches a high export price."

One of the other men then rose to his feet. "Sir, I am Samuel, and I am in charge of a group of people who make cooking pots. Visitors to Salem are always pleased to buy them from us." Others then spoke up, and soon wine, ivory, and wood for building purposes were added to the list of potential trade items.

"Then we shall first concentrate on increasing our exports," Mel said. "Let me ask you a question: is Egypt one of our trading partners?"

It was Sirach's turn to speak again. "Sir, the Egyptians are wealthy and powerful, and so far we have remained on friendly terms with them. They are always willing to buy the goods we are able to produce."

"Then I shall make contact with them," Mel replied. "I shall ask them for troops to protect us against those who invade and steal from our people.[19] Also, I shall seek help from them to enable work on completing the city walls to commence. In the meantime, I ask you the Elders, and others like you who run businesses, to produce as much as you can for export to Egypt, to help pay for whatever assistance they agree to give us."

The Elders took this as a cue that it was time for them to leave. Before departing, Sirach thanked Mel for the audience and the food. He seemed relieved that they had been given the opportunity to voice their concerns, and that Mel had promised to take action to address them.

When they had gone, Mel sent for his Secretary. He was surprised to find that Daniel was much younger than were the other senior members of his staff. "Lord Melchizedek, I am at your service, what do you wish of me?"

"Firstly, tell me something about yourself. You carry a lot of responsibility for such a young man," Mel said.

"Sir, it is true that I am but twenty-five years old, but I have spent many years being taught by priests and scholars. The previous ruler gave me this job because I can both speak and write in several of the languages used in this part of the world."

"Excellent," replied Mel. "Well, I want you to write a letter to Pharaoh Mentuhotep of Egypt.[20] Firstly, I need to introduce myself as the new King and High Priest of Salem. Then I wish to extend my greetings to him, along with my hopes that the two of us can work together in peace and cooperation. Next, I need to suggest that we make a trade agreement so that we can increase our exports to Egypt. Finally, we need help to complete our defensive wall, and troops to protect our citizens."

"I can compose a letter in the style appropriate for a communication between two Heads of State, including all that you have requested, and will then bring it to you for your signature," responded Daniel. "If it is your wish, I can give the letter to a reliable messenger for delivery to the Pharaoh's court. He can then await any reply that is forthcoming, and bring it back to you."

"This is very good," replied Mel. "You are very accomplished, and I can see why you were given this job."

The secretary was clearly pleased with this compliment, and withdrew to complete his task. The afternoon was not yet over, so Mel decided to change from his royal robes into more simple clothing, and explore more of the city on his own before the sun went down. Hopefully, he would not be recognized, and would be able to move around unhindered.

Later, back in the Palace and enjoying his evening meal, Mel reflected on the events of this, his first day in office. Despite his concerns that he would prove to be incompetent, perhaps even a fraud, he had already managed to accomplish something and had gained the confidence of those around him. This had at least bought him some time, but he now needed to deliver on his promises. Would he be able to do so?

He would surely find out over the days and weeks to come.

Chapter 8

THE HIGH PRIEST

The next morning Mel prepared himself to investigate what he could do to fulfill his parallel role of High Priest. After breaking his fast with the fruit and nuts that were again left for him, he selected what he hoped would be suitable priestly attire. The choice available to him was limited, so he donned a full-length white robe, and a cloak that he thought must have been dyed with the expensive purple murex color the elders had mentioned the previous day. He could find no alternative head covering to the black and gold helmet he wore as King.

Descending to the lower floor, he was met by his Secretary, who was carrying the letter he had prepared for sending to Pharaoh Mentuhotep. Daniel read aloud what he had written and, as he had intimated earlier, he was obviously accomplished in the skills of diplomatic communication. "Excellent," said Mel. "I am prepared to sign this so that it can be dispatched without delay." This was not quite as easy as Mel had anticipated. He was handed a pen fashioned from a reed, and a small pot of ink made from soot and vegetable gum. With some trial, and more than a little error, he eventually managed a rather clumsy 'Melchizedek' along the bottom of what he assumed was a sheet of parchment.

"I have the messenger standing by and ready to leave once I have carefully placed this letter in a protective cylinder," Daniel explained.

Mel asked him: "How long do you think it will be before we hear back from the Pharaoh?" If he had been naively anticipating the reply would be received within days, or even a week or two, he was in for a surprise.

"Thebes is more than a thousand kilometers from here," said Daniel. "The messenger will first travel to Jaffa and there wait for a ship that is sailing to Alexandria in Egypt. He will then try to obtain a passage on a boat that will sail up the Nile to the capital city. It might mean that he has to change vessels more than once to get to his destination, or he could be lucky and find one that is going all the way. Once there, he will have to wait for the Pharaoh to respond, and then make the return journey. If all goes well, we may see him return in little more than a month from now."

But Daniel had not quite finished. "There are dangers and risks involved. He may be attacked, robbed, or even killed by bandits. A dishonest ship's captain might take all his possessions and dump him on a remote part of the coast—or even into the sea. Then of course there is the weather, and the chance a shipwreck."

This did nothing to inspire Mel's optimism that outside help to strengthen Salem's security situation would be forthcoming quickly, if at all. He would have to give thought to initiating some interim measures in the meantime. However, he simply replied: "Thank you, Daniel, just tell the messenger to do his best, and that I shall pray to our god El Elyon that he will have a safe journey."

With that his Secretary withdrew, and Mel sought out the Chief of Servants. "Obadiah," he said. "I wish to make my first official visit to the Temple. Before I can consider taking any actions, it is important to first investigate what already takes place there. It will help to make this occasion more formal if the people know that I am going to their place of worship, and that you are accompanying me."

"I shall be honored to do so," said Obadiah. "Although the Temple is only a short distance away, may I suggest that we ride there on horses to make this a ceremonial visit. I can ask the Groomsman to prepare two mounts, and send some servants into the streets to spread the word that you will be coming."

Mel readily agreed to this, but they decided to wait a short while before leaving, to allow time for the announcement of his intended visit to spread, and for the horses to be prepared. It also gave him a chance to give further thought to what his mission would entail. Archangel Michael had told him of the apostasy that was starting to spread, and of the increasing worship of idols and false gods, including Ba'al. His mission was to preach monotheism and the worship of the one true god, El Elyon.

It was not long before Obadiah announced that the horses were ready for them, and that the servants had returned after publicizing Mel's pending visit. They mounted up and made their way slowly along the road to the Temple, which was situated only a few hundred meters to the north of the Palace. Just as it was when Mel entered the city two days ago, people lined the street waving and cheering as he went by.

After a few minutes, they arrived at the Temple. This was not the imposing edifice that would be built by King Solomon over a millennium from now, but a relatively modest building. They dismounted and entered the premises, leaving their horses with the Groomsman who had been following behind them.

Once inside, they were greeted with due reverence by two attendants who were permanently stationed there to guard the Temple and receive the donations. Mel saw that the building comprised a broad room with an open porch and courtyard. He was surprised to see there were tables and seats in the outside area, and that some men were present who appeared to be counting money. When he queried this, Obadiah explained that these were bankers who changed money for those who needed to visit foreign lands, and visitors who needed local currency. They were not always honest in their dealings and, like unscrupulous tax collectors, they were generally disliked by the rest of the population.

"If this is so," Mel asked Obadiah, "Why are the money changers allowed to trade here?"

"Sir, they are tolerated because they pay rental for their places in the courtyard, and this income helps to maintain the Temple." Mel decided he would give this some thought later but, for now, he needed to continue his survey of the premises.

Within the main enclosed area was an altar used for sacrifices and, behind that, a small recess where the most precious cult objects were kept—the 'Holy of Holies'. Leading off from each side of the room were antechambers, one for the High Priest's exclusive use and another for the guards. [21]

Mel was so preoccupied with exploring the Temple that he had failed to notice that the men and women who had been cheering him outside were now streaming into the building. It was becoming crowded, so he made his way to the altar, the only place that had been left clear for him. He had not prepared himself for any speeches during this first visit, but it became increasingly obvious that something was expected of him.

As soon as he had reached the little sanctuary and turned to face the gathering, the background hubbub faded away and a respectful silence prevailed. Rather tamely, all Mel could think of to say as an opening statement was: "I greet you all, thank you for your welcome. I have been sent by El Elyon to be your High Priest."

A man from the crowd then spoke up. "Lord Melchizedek, we have anticipated your coming and are pleased to once again have a spiritual leader. But firstly, to prove that you are who you say you are, would you please show us your Badge of Priesthood." Judging from the murmurs of agreement from the crowd, this was something that everyone wanted to see.

Mel tried to conceal his embarrassment at this request, but realized the necessity of confirming his credentials if he was going to achieve anything. "Very well," he said. He pulled open the top part of his robe to reveal the serpent scales on his chest. Although he was still sure that he could feel the first swelling of horns and tail, he did not choose to mention them here. There was an audible gasp from the people, followed by noises of approval. "Are you convinced by what you have seen?" he asked.

The man who had made the request answered on behalf of all. "Certainly Sir, thank you. You are indeed the one for whom we have been waiting. What do you wish of us?"

"I have been sent here because many of you have turned away from El Elyon and started to worship false gods, including the evil Ba'al and his mistress, Asherah. Sacrifices have been made to idols and to fertility deities." [22] Mel looked around and saw several in the audience looking distinctly uncomfortable. He continued, "Your visitors and messengers will have told you of the terrible destruction that has occurred in Mesopotamia, to the south of here. A great flood has destroyed every living thing there because the people had turned to sin and apostasy. Canaan has been spared, at least for the moment, to give you all a final chance to cease your evil ways and worship only El Elyon."

Mel was surprised by the way the words flowed from his mouth. He had not been conscious of formulating these in his own mind; it was as if somebody else was speaking their words through him. He continued: "I know that Salem is troubled by invaders who come and steal your possessions. These people have their own gods, and try to prove their superiority over the one true God. Perhaps you feel that our deity is not protecting you, and therefore turn in desperation to other gods who you think will keep you safe." He glanced at the faces of those in the congregation, and noticed that many were nodding in silent agreement.

"El Elyon has sent me to you as your High Priest, and to deliver you from the power of Belial, the devil. I say to you, worship only the one true God, and ask him for help; he is sure to hear your prayers.[23] Stop making sacrifices to your idols and false gods—you should know by now that they have not helped you. El Elyon does not wish for such sacrifices, but only for your exclusive loyalty and devotion. Burnt offerings are a waste of good food that can be eaten or sold. So save your money and offer yourselves in service to him, instead of your animals.[24] But still bring gifts of food and money to the Temple to help maintain it, and provide for the poor."

Mel paused to let this message sink in, and allow the people to exchange comments among themselves. He carefully watched their reactions. Whilst these indicated some surprise at the exhortation to cease the practice of sacrificing, there were also obvious signs of relief that their meager livestocks would not be further depleted by the need to fulfill sacrificial obligations.

Resuming his address, he said, "I was also sent by El Elyon to be your King. Yesterday, I had a meeting with your Elders to discuss the situation in Salem, and we agreed on the need to increase the security for those who live both inside and outside the city gates. This morning I sent a letter to Pharaoh Mentuhotep of Egypt, introducing myself and stating my wish that we can work together in peaceful cooperation. I suggested that it would be in our mutual interest to increase trade, and I asked him if he could provide help so that we can complete the city wall. We also need to protect those who do not live within its perimeter." [25]

Before continuing, he asked if anybody wished to ask a question. One man spoke up, "Lord Melchizedek, I am Joel, a shoemaker. Yes, we do have a good opportunity to trade with visitors who pass through this area, but many of them are reluctant to come here because of the fear of being attacked and robbed. We have often discussed the need to complete the city wall, and to make this a safe area for all, but we have not had the money to accomplish this after our last Chieftain spent it on his own invasion force." There were mutterings of agreement from the rest of the congregation.

Mel was confident that he understood the issues facing this community, and was sure that he could initiate appropriate action. "Very well, Joel, I hear what you have to say. We do not have to wait for the Pharaoh's response before starting to take action for ourselves. If we can stop being robbed by invaders, we can sell more goods and start to accumulate funds to pay for the building work.[26] I have already stated that we should not waste money on needless animal sacrifice.

This unexpected gathering of ordinary citizens gave Mel the chance to solicit help to achieve a plan that was forming in his mind. Addressing all present he said, "I ask all able-bodied men here to form a neighborhood watch platoon. If a rota is drawn up for teams of volunteers to patrol in four-hour shifts both day and night, those who try to sneak in and rob us will find that they are repelled. The more people who take part, then the less times anyone will need to go out on patrol. What do you say to this?"

It was clear from the reaction that this idea had been received with enthusiasm. One man raised his hand to speak. "Sir, I am Baruch. I served as a guardsman for many years before I became a farmer. If it is your wish, I shall be pleased to organize the patrols and recruit as many men I can to participate in them."

"Thank you, Baruch," responded Mel. "I shall certainly bless your effort and pray for the safety of the platoon, but it is the people who will take part who must agree to your leadership." He turned to the congregation and said, "Raise your hand if you wish Baruch to organize the watch patrols and, if so, you agree to his leadership." A sea of hands appeared in front of him. "You now have your mandate, Baruch, so please commence your work as soon as you are able, and report your progress to me at the Palace."

Having achieved this agreement, Mel decided that he had just one more topic to raise, before he made his exit. Addressing the congregation he said, "I have seen those in the courtyard who exchange money. Because they provide revenue for the Temple, I shall not immediately ban them so long as they provide an honest service and do not cheat their customers. If you have any complaint against one of them, report this to me during my visits here. If the complaint is justified, then the culprit will be banned from doing any further business in this place. This also apples to any business man or woman; only honest trade will be permitted in Salem."

He now brought this, his first visit to the Temple, to a close. "Brothers and sisters, I shall leave you now but remember what I have told you. Remain loyal to El Elyon, worship only him. Your false gods did nothing to help you, but he has sent me to give you spiritual guidance. I shall visit this Temple regularly. If you wish to discuss your faith or your religious practices with me, please tell the temple attendants and they will give me the list of names when I visit."

With that, Mel left the Temple. He and Obadiah collected their horses from the Groomsman, and made their way back to the Palace. Once there, he reflected on this, his first day as High Priest. It caused him some surprise how easily the role seemed to have come to him, just as it did yesterday with his initiation into the duties of kingship. Was this really him, acting on his own initiative, or was he merely a convenient physical body through which another power was working?

Chapter 9

PROGRESS

The days passed. Mel devoted all the time he could to learning about the people of Salem and their activities. If he was to be an effective leader, then he needed to be kept informed. In order to help with achieving this, and to maintain his public profile, he held weekly sessions in the throne room at the Palace where anyone could attend and speak. His Secretary, Daniel, would be there taking notes so that a record could be kept of the issues raised, along with the actions that were proposed to deal with them. These minutes could be referred to at future meetings so that progress reports could be given.

He was also required to judge cases of alleged breaches of the law, and disputes that the parties involved had failed to resolve among themselves. Although Mel was not very confident in this role, as King of this part of the world he was the ultimate authority whether or not he wished to be so. Often the verdicts involved little more than logic and common sense, but some cases were more difficult and required legal knowledge that he did not have. At such times it was necessary to adjourn the hearing and consult with others for advice. On many occasions Daniel proved to have an

Reincarnation

encyclopedic knowledge of the existing law that proved invaluable, so that these more difficult cases could usually be resolved.

What Mel did find very uncomfortable was how to punish those who had been found guilty. He had an aversion to capital punishment, and vowed to avoid using this if at all possible. On the other hand, he thought that prolonged prison sentences were both a drain on public resources, and did little to rehabilitate the criminals. He was relieved that, in most cases, he was able to discipline the culprits by either fining them or sentencing them to periods of unpaid public service.

It was important that he did not neglect his duties as High Priest. Although other activities prevented him from making daily visits to the Temple, he let it be known that he would be present each Monday and Friday morning until noon. There he would lead the prayers to El Elyon, sing hymns, and remind the people to worship only the one true God. As was the custom at that time in the Middle East, Mel was asked to perform purifications and exorcisms. He also laid his hands on those who were sick, whilst calling on the Lord to heal them.[27] Although he had received no training in these duties, an understanding of what to do and how to do it just came naturally to him, in a way he could not explain.

Mel decided not to try to start any major new ventures for the moment, but to concentrate on accomplishing what had already been proposed. He was confident that exploiting the potential for increased trade was a key target. It was a distinct advantage that Salem was situated where it was, on a crossroads where travelers needed to refresh themselves and purchase supplies for their journeys. He hoped that the revenue from this would provide a budget surplus of funds that could be used to recommence building work, and pay for other improvements in the city.

This was, however, something of a circular issue. The number of visitors would increase if there was confidence that they would remain safe and secure whilst they were here. But money was needed to pay for the city walls and a permanent security force, in order to provide this safe environment. Mel's hope was that the scheme to recruit volunteers for the neighborhood watch patrols

54

would be a successful interim measure. He received welcome news on this matter when Baruch came to the Palace a week later, to make his first report.

"Lord Melchizedek, the recruitment has gone exceedingly well," he said. "The able-bodied men of the city and surrounding areas have agreed that going out on patrol for four hours every week or two is a small price to pay to protect their homes and possessions. I already have a force of more than one hundred and fifty volunteers. Even in this short time we have prevented several small groups of raiders from succeeding in their attempts to steal from us."

"This is excellent news, Baruch. What have you done with raiders when you have caught them?" asked Mel.

"Sir, it would tie up our manpower and resources if we were to put these people in jail. Instead, we take their weapons and threaten them with severe punishment if they are caught here again. If they try to fight us, we fight back vigorously. Then we send them back to where they came from, telling them to inform the leaders of their tribes that we will not tolerate such invasions."

Mel was greatly encouraged by the successes that had already been achieved. "I am very pleased with this; you have done well. Please pass my congratulations to the men. I shall continue to pray for their safety, and lead similar prayers when I officiate in the Temple. In the meantime, do continue with this good work that is already benefitting us all."

Baruch left, clearly happy that his news had been so well received by his King, and Mel concluded that he was obviously the right person for this task. This left him to wonder if military help from the Egyptians would indeed be needed, should it be offered. But then, in the future, there may be bigger battles to fight than just the skirmishes with small bands of nomadic raiders. It would be useful to receive an update on the treasury finances to see if the situation had improved, so he sent for the Chancellor.

"Jacob, I hear that the neighborhood patrols are already reducing the robberies that were previously being carried out by the raiding parties. Has this led to an improvement in our income?"

"My Lord, the revenue from tithes and taxes resulting from trade has indeed increased recently, thanks to our strengthened security. We have been able to pay the Palace staff their full wages for the first time in many weeks."

"This is good, Jacob. Do we yet have sufficient surplus to re-commence building work on the city walls?"

"Sir, at this time we do not have enough funding to employ more than just a few men, but I shall budget some money for this project if it is your wish. If our situation improves still further, I can advise you that the workforce can be increased."

"Very well, Jacob, let us do this. I shall speak with the fore-man of the Elders to see if we can make a start on this work."

When the Chancellor had departed, Mel asked his Chief Servant, Obadiah, to find Sirach and request him to come to the Palace after the midday meal. When the Elder arrived, Mel told him that it would now be possible to make a modest start on the walls, and asked if he would be able to recruit some stonemasons and builders to do the work.

"Sir, this is welcome news. I knew that the security patrols had already brought about an improvement, and my fellow Elders who are manufacturers or merchants have reported increased business. We are in touch with the craftsmen that are needed for the building, and I know they will be glad of the chance to work."

"Very well, Sirach, I leave it to you to take the necessary ac-tion. It will be good for the local people and the visitors to see that something is happening. Also, it will show those who wish to invade us that we are making it more difficult for them to do so. Please keep me informed on the progress, and consult with Chancellor Jacob on a weekly basis to check the amount of fund-ing available."

After the Elder had departed, Mel retired to his room to relax and reflect on what had been achieved in such a relatively short time. Was he being lulled into a sense that it would always be as easy as it had been up to now, or were far more severe tests to come? The thought that had entered his mind when speaking in the Temple returned. He had been surprised at the words that had flowed from his mouth, and he likewise now wondered how he had been able to make so much progress on a number of issues. Were the words that he had spoken, and the actions he had taken, really his own, or was he being manipulated by a higher power, just like a puppet?

He was thankful that he had made no further arrangements for the remainder of the day, and that he now had this rare period of quiet time to himself. His mind strayed back to the very start of this adventure, to his father Nir and Uncle Noah, and them telling him that he had been chosen for a special mission. Why him, he wondered? Then there was the discovery of the Badge of Priesthood on his chest. The very thought of this made him feel uncomfortable, and especially that he might also develop horns and a tail.

Making himself more comfortable in his chair, Mel closed his eyes and reviewed what had happened to him up to now. His very birth had been unusual, precipitating him into the world as a young child rather than a baby. Then to be told that he had been sent by El Elyon to fulfill a mission, but without any initial explanation as to what this would be. He had aged unnaturally quickly, and been whisked away by Archangel Michael to the Garden of Eden to escape the flood that engulfed a large part of the world. Before Michael had left, he had told him he would later be taken to Salem to become King and High Priest, and that he would have the task of delivering the people from the powers of evil.

Finally, he had been visited again by Michael and brought to within sight of Salem. Little more of his mission had been revealed to him, but only that the El Elyon would supply all the help and guidance he needed. Is this why he had managed to achieve so much? Was he just the Lord's mouthpiece, without using any of his own skills or judgments? Once again the thought that he might be being manipulated in this way filled him with disappointment and helplessness. If all his actions were being determined, Mel wondered if he would have the power to override these, should he feel inclined to do so. But then, even if this were possible, would it be wise?

He resolved to keep this thought in his mind, in case a situation arose where his own decision might differ from that into which he felt he was being pushed. If El Elyon was benevolent and loving, then surely he would not be imposing his almighty will on people. Although this may mean there would be no evil in the world, there would also be no freedom. It was more likely that he was guiding them along the correct path, but leaving them free to deviate from it if that was their choice. However, those who did would have to accept the consequences of doing so. Is this not the way caring parents try to bring up their children?

What continued to trouble Mel was the sense that there was something unreal about his situation. Yes, he was here in Salem. Yes, he was interacting with people and making things happen. Yes, he was made of flesh and blood, and needed food and water to survive. If he pinched himself, it hurt. It was just that there was a feeling he was like an actor on a stage. Would somebody eventually call "cut" and the play would stop, allowing him to revert to his real self? What would this "real self" then be? Although Nir had explained his origins, the fact that he was the product of a virgin birth did little to reassure him that he was a genuine human being in every sense.

His relaxed repose in a comfortable chair was propelling him into that creative and uncensored state of consciousness that exists between waking and sleeping. Images of a different landscape drifted into his mind. Instead of Salem, he was floating above a large, modern town with many streets and houses. Thousands of people were bustling backwards and forwards, like bees on a piece of honeycomb just removed from a hive. Mel sensed that somewhere amongst this throng was a person special to him. Yes, it was a woman. He had been so busy dealing with men in this patriarchal society, that he had been temporarily oblivious of his need for female company. [28]

Searching frantically among the figures milling below him, he tried to pick out somebody he would recognize. Spotting a woman among the crowds, he wondered—is it her? No. There's another one—is that the person I am seeking? No. Perhaps that girl over there? No. Then this one; that one; maybe her . . . . Sleep mercifully came to his rescue.

But then the dreams started, and the vision continued. He was still floating above the houses, and suddenly spotted one building that looked familiar. Not only that, but a young woman was standing in the doorway. Was this the one he was seeking? He called out to her, "Hello, hello. This is Mel. I am up here." There was no indication that he had been heard, so he shouted at the top of his voice, "Look upwards, this is Mel; please look up." His words were carried away on the wind, and the woman walked down the path and into the street. Nobody heard him; nobody saw him. He was filled with a feeling of sadness.

Mel became aware of a knocking sound. He tried to ignore it. The knocking continued. A voice then said, "My Lord, are you alright?" The vision he was experiencing quickly faded, and he slowly opened his eyes. With an effort he regained consciousness, and remembered where he was.

"Yes, I was just resting," he replied. "You may enter the room."

A Palace servant came in. "Sir, your evening meal has been ready for some time now, and we were concerned that you might be ill."

Mel realized that he must have been asleep. Had he been dreaming, or had he really been transported back into another existence? This was not the first time he had been faced with this dilemma, and it would not be the last. "I shall come down for the meal presently," he said. "Your concern is appreciated." With that, he splashed his face with cold water to try and revive himself, and then descended to the private dining room for the food that had been prepared for him. He would be eating alone tonight.

Chapter 10

ABRAHAM

Terah, who was a descendent of Noah, lived in the city of Ur in the Chaldeans, which only later became part of Babylonia.[29] The population worshiped a variety of gods, with the chief deity being Ningal, a moon-goddess. Terah earned a good living from making idols, which he then sold in his own shop.[30] One day he left his son Abraham in charge of the store, but the boy was not comfortable with the idea of worshipping these objects made of wood and stone. Whilst his father was out, a woman came into the store and said to the boy, "Here is some flour, please feed the idols with it."

Abraham did not want to upset one of his father's customers, so he simply replied, "Thank you for the food, madam. I shall serve it to the statues when it is the appropriate time to do so." Once the customer had left, he became so enraged that he staged a mock battle between the idols. He placed a stick into the hands of the largest, and destroyed all the rest.

When Terah returned and saw the smashed idols, he was furious. He shouted at the boy, "What happened to all my handiwork?

"A woman brought some flour to feed the idols. Before I could give it to them, there was a battle between the different deities, and only one survived," his son replied.

Terah knew that the boy was not telling the truth, but was mocking him. He said angrily, "But they are statues and not living beings, how then could they fight each other?"

The young Abraham responded to the question with one of his own. "If they are just made of wood and stone, then why do people bow down and worship them?"

Whilst this unexpected response did little to consol Terah after his loss of many weeks of hard work, it did resonate with some thoughts of his own that had still been at the embryo stage. His business, lucrative as it was, was helping to perpetuate religious beliefs and practices that, deep down, seemed increasingly alien to him. He said to his son, "Your actions have cost me a lot of money, and you must be punished for this. But your question reinforces ideas I have been having that it may be time for me to start a new life."

It was not many days later that Terah announced to his family that they were going to leave Ur and travel to the north. It would be a spiritual journey for him personally and, although the boy did not fully appreciate it at the time, it would also be so for Abraham. Terah needed to put his idolatry behind him, literally and figuratively, and seek a new path. Once they had completed their preparations the patriarch, along with other family members, and their servants, began their journey northwards. For much of the time they travelled close to the Euphrates River. After many months, they had completed nearly one thousand kilometers, reaching the town of Haran, where they decided to set up residence.

They remained in this place until Terah died, several years later. Shortly thereafter, Abraham was aware that the one true God, in whom he believed, was speaking to him. He was given the instruction to: "Leave this land, and your father's home, and go to a country that I am going to show you." The message continued, "I will give you many descendents, and they will become a great nation."

Although Abraham did not understand what might be in store for him, he had no wish to refuse this directive from his Lord. If this is what he had been asked to do, by the one he trusted, then he would do it. Adopting the role of patriarch, now that he was the eldest male, he prepared his remaining family members, servants, and slaves, and gathered together the considerable wealth that they had accumulated by this time. Only as they were departing from Haran did Abraham receive another message, this time telling him that their destination would be Canaan.

Their journey now took them south, to the west of the River Jordon. They stopped first at Shechem in Samaria, before moving on and setting up camp near Bethel, which is only about sixteen kilometers north of Salem where Melchizedek was currently residing. Although neither he nor Abraham knew it at this time, fate would one day bring them together not too far from this place. Before then, however, Abraham literally had some battles of his own to fight.

The travelers expected to settle down and make Bethel their permanent home in Canaan. Abraham had received another message from God, repeating the promise that he would be given this land, and would have many descendents. In time, this greater family of those faithful to the one God would replace the apostate idol-worshipers that currently inhabited the country. They had not been there long, however, when it became clear that a great famine had already begun in Canaan. Because the party had had neither the time to plant their own crops and reap the harvest, nor buy cattle and allow them to breed, they were going to suffer far more than would the local people.

Abraham therefore called together his family and servants, and said, "Although I have been called to come to this place, if we stay here we shall surely die of starvation. We must therefore take up our journey again and travel south to Egypt, where there will be food to eat." Whilst this news came as a disappointment to the others after their years of wanderings, the inevitability of the need to move on was reluctantly accepted.

The patriarch's entourage had been steadily growing over time. This was partly due to his growing reputation as a God-fearing man, which led people to want to join his group and follow him. In addition, his wealth meant that he could afford to hire more helpers as he needed them, to work in the settlement and tend the animals. The ensemble that broke camp and travelled south to Egypt was thus considerably larger than that which had left Ur in Babylonia all those years ago.

Once they had arrived in Egypt, it was not long before Abraham found favor with the Pharaoh. His wealth, possessions and followers increased still further as a result. But this was not to last for long. The patriarch had used some trickery that involved his beautiful wife, Sarai. He had deceived the monarch into believing that she was available to enter his royal harem. It was, however, against the law for a married woman to be so recruited if her husband was still alive. When the Pharaoh found out, he was angry and expelled Abraham and all his party from his kingdom.

The group, now several hundred in number, set off back to Canaan, where the famine was at last coming to an end. Among Abraham's greater family was his nephew, Lot. Because they had acquired so much livestock between them that needed grazing land, the two men decided to part company so that they could each lead their respective animals to pastures in different parts of the country. Abraham moved to Hebron, which is only about thirty kilometers south of Salem. Lot eventually settled in the city of Sodom, to the east of the southern part of the Dead Sea.

He had not been there very long, however, when a war broke out between rival kings who ruled over small nations in this part of the world. Although Lot was not involved in the fighting, he and others in his party were taken into captivity when Sodom was defeated. There he would no doubt have remained for a long time, perhaps suffering an even worse fate, had not one of his servants escaped. Knowing that his master was related to Abraham, who had already achieved a reputation as a person who was not only righteous, but as a man of influence, the servant made the journey to Hebron as fast as he could.

When he found Abraham, he told him, "Lord, my master Lot and his family have been captured by Chedorlaomer, King of Elam, and the other victorious kings. The city of Sodom has been occupied by the conquerors, and your relatives are being held captive there."

"Have others also been taken prisoner?" asked Abraham.

"Yes sir, there are many women as well as men being held there. I do not know what will eventually happen to them."

"You have done well to find me and tell me this," said Abraham. "I shall gather together a fighting force to go and rescue them. Would you like to be a part of this?"

"Indeed, my lord, I would," the servant replied. "I have always been treated well by your nephew, and many of my friends are amongst those captured."

This was an opportunity for Abraham to prove himself as a successful warrior as well as a spiritual leader. His following had grown so large that he was able to assemble an army of three hundred and eighteen fighting men from his camp, and they all set off for Sodom. When they were at the outskirts of the city, he divided his forces into smaller groups. The area was heavily wooded. At night they used the trees as cover, and attacked the enemy on several fronts, so that each of the kings were struck at the same time. [31]

The attack was successful, and the city was liberated. All the enemies were defeated, and the survivors fled to the north. Abraham's fighting men pursued them until they were beyond Damascus, to make sure they did not return. Lot, along with all the other prisoners, were freed, and the treasures and other possessions that had been taken from them were recovered. In addition, there was a large amount of bounty that the enemy had accumulated as the spoils of previous wars. Abraham was indeed now a successful warrior king. He had shown great courage and resourcefulness with his limited resources, and he had maintained faith in his God.

On their return journey south to Hebron, Abraham and his weary troops passed through the Kidron Valley, which is situated between Salem and the Mount of Olives. There they were met by King Bera of Sodom, who was now free after the occupying forces had been defeated. He had lost no time in travelling north in order to personally thank the man who had defeated his enemies.

As soon as Bera saw Abraham at the head of his forces, he hailed him and said, "Sir, I am eternally grateful to you and your men for liberating my city, and setting the captives free. As a reward, please keep for yourself all booty that has been recovered."

Abraham replied, "King Bera, what I have done is in response to the calling of the one Lord. He has strengthened my hand and let me release my nephew Lot, along with you and your people." He continued, "It is generous of you to invite me to keep the recovered riches, but I must decline. To accept this would be a reward from an earthly king, but I am content to be rewarded only by the King in heaven. However, let my fighting men have what they wish, as their share of the spoils of war."

But Sodom's king was not the only royal personage who would come and meet Abraham whilst he was in the Valley. Successful but exhausted from their efforts, the victorious army and its commander were now in need of some rest and refreshment.

Chapter II

PHAROAH'S REPLY

"Lord Melchizedek, the messenger has returned with a response from Pharaoh Mentuhotep of Egypt." It was his Secretary Daniel.

"This is good news," Mel responded, "He has completed his journey much quicker than expected."

"Indeed he has, Sir. He was accompanied on his passage homeward by a nobleman provided by the Pharaoh. This was to ensure that he was given immediate transportation at all stages, and thus there were no delays."

Mel thought that this was a very magnanimous gesture by the leader of one of the most powerful nations at that time, and he hoped that this would be reflected in the reply he was about to receive. "Are you able to translate the message from Pharaoh?" he asked.

"Sir, I am confident that I can understand the essence of what has been written," Daniel said, "And the nobleman is a well educated man; he will help me if I struggle with any of the hieroglyphics."

"I would like to meet this man, so that I can thank him personally," Mel replied. "Is he here now?"

His Secretary beckoned to a figure standing in the shadows near the door. The man had a milky brown skin tone, and was wearing a white, one-piece tunic that came to just below his knees. Around his neck was a broad collar with gold edges, and decorated with a pattern of red and blue oblongs. Cuffs around the lower part of his otherwise bare arms were of a similar design. Daniel provided the introduction:

"Lord Melchizedek, this is Hannu, who was the messenger's companion during the journey home." [32]

The Egyptian bowed respectfully, and repeated Mel's regal name. "Hannu, thank you for accompanying my messenger on his homeward journey, and ensuring that he arrived safely and quickly," said Mel. "I am grateful to both you and your Pharaoh. You must avail yourself of our hospitality whilst you are with us in Salem."

There was a short pause whilst Daniel quietly translated any part of the message that Hannu may not have understood. He then conveyed to Mel the nobleman's reply. "Hannu says it is an honor to be here and, in turn, he thanks you for your welcome. When he returns to Egypt, he will gladly take back to his king any further message you may have."

With the formalities now over, Mel was eager to know what Pharaoh's response would be. In his own message he had expressed his wish that the two countries could work together in peace and cooperation. Also, he had suggested a trade agreement to boost exports, and requested help to improve Salem's defenses. Daniel unrolled a papyrus scroll and began to translate what had been written there, sometimes conferring with Hannu to confirm his accuracy.

"Pharaoh Mentuhotep thanks you for your message and your good wishes. He agrees that there should be peace and cooperation between us, and would welcome a trade agreement. He especially values the murex dye we produce; he also needs wood for building and ivory for the manufacture of decorative objects. To help the speedy transportation of goods, he will create a protected corridor from the borders of Egypt to his capital at Thebes."

So far this seemed to be a friendly and potentially lucrative response, but Mel was keen to hear what was written about the all-important matter of defense.

Daniel continued: "The Pharaoh understands the strategic importance of Salem, due to its position on major north-south, east-west trading routes. It is a place where travelers, including those from Egypt, can rest and obtain essential goods for their journeys. Thus it is important that it be kept safe and secure, so that visitors can be sure they will not be attacked or robbed." Again, this seemed very promising but, thought Mel, would Mentuhotep provide any manpower to help with the defenses? He prompted his Secretary to proceed.

"I regret that I cannot supply you with troops to help you fight your enemies," the message read. "We have a limited number of soldiers, and threats of our own to deal with. Invasions from Nubia, Libya, Syria, and other countries near our borders, could occur at any time. It would be risky for me to send men to a place too far away from our country to be available quickly, in the event of an attack from one of our adversaries."

It was disappointing to hear this, but then came some rather better news. Daniel continued, "I am prepared to send you some military advisors to help train your own fighting men. In addition, if you wish, I can send you some engineers and laborers to help you with the building of your city walls."

The message ended with salutations, and an invitation to send any return message back with nobleman Hannu. Mel now needed time to think, and to consult with others. He said, "Thank you. I shall indeed compose a reply to Pharaoh Mentuhotep, once I have discussed this with my advisers." Addressing Daniel he added, "Please ensure that Hannu is availed of all the hospitality we can offer him, until it is time for him to return."

Once he was alone, Mel reviewed the situation. Whilst it would have been very good to have Egyptian troops to help him, he understood the reasons why this was not to be. Whether or not Salem could maintain its own regular army would depend on how much money was available to pay the soldiers. The recent improvement in revenue from trade, and the promise of increased exports to Egypt, made the likelihood of being able to maintain a permanent defense force a distinct possibility. He needed to call a gathering of all those who were involved in the running of the city, in order to discuss strategy and agree on a response to the Pharaoh.

Mel sent messages to those he had come to regard as his team of inner cabinet ministers. There was Jacob the Chancellor, Sirach the Chief Elder, Baruch the Patrol Organizer, and Daniel his versatile Secretary. He invited them to join him for today's evening meal, after which they would discuss Salem's economic and security situation.

Once they had finished eating, and were enjoying the single goblet of wine that he had restricted them to before the business meeting, Mel summarized the message he had received from Mentuhotep. "Let us deal firstly with the offer to help train our own fighting men." Addressing Baruch who, as an ex guardsman, was an appropriate person to lead such an army, if one were to be commissioned, he asked, "Would you welcome such assistance from Egypt?"

"Sir," replied Baruch, "At this time we just have the volunteer patrols. They are doing an excellent job but, up to now, we have only had to deal with small raiding parties. We remain vulnerable to a co-ordinated attack by a sizeable invading force. Salem will be a much safer place if we can set up a permanent company of men, even if initially modest in numbers." He then added, "It is many years since I was an active soldier, so it would be very helpful to have the experience that Egyptian instructors would bring."

"Thank you Baruch." Mel now turned to Chancellor Jacob. He asked him, "Can we afford to immediately start recruiting full-time soldiers?"

"Our financial situation has improved significantly in the last two months," Jacob replied. "This is mainly due to the increased trade with those who pass through our city, now that the word has spread that they will be protected from robbers." He continued, "The news you have just been given of a desire by the Egyptians to take more goods from us, gives me confidence that we are in a position to fund our own army, provided we start small and only expand when we have the means to pay for it."

Mel addressed Baruch again. "Then it would seem right that we start to form our own permanent fighting force. I appoint you as Commander, if you are prepared to take this role."

"It would be an honor to serve you and Salem in this way," he replied but, as King, you would be the Commander in Chief of the armed forces, and be expected to lead them into battle. My position would be as your lieutenant, and I would gladly support you whilst holding this rank."

This came as a shock to Mel; he had not foreseen that he would also have to be a military leader. His duties as both King and High Priest had so far been accomplished much better than he had initially expected. But to have lead troops into battle—that was something completely new. He felt completely ignorant and inadequate to even make an attempt at military command, but he realized that he must not let this be obvious to those who looked up to him as their divinely-appointed ruler.

He paused for a moment whilst these thoughts raced through his mind, hoping that his hesitation would not be seen as a weakness. "Yes," he eventually said. "Of course, if and when it becomes necessary to lead the troops in anger, I shall be there." He continued, "Lieutenant Baruch, before you start to recruit the men, please consult with Chancellor Jacob to draw up a budget based on what we can afford, and restrict numbers so as not to exceed this. I do not want a repetition of what happened with the previous ruler of Salem, who bankrupted the city when he went off to try and conquer foreign lands."

"Yes Sir, I am sure that none of us would want that," agreed Baruch. "It is certain that at least some of those who currently participating in the voluntary patrols will welcome the chance to become paid, full-time soldiers. I shall start their basic training whilst awaiting the arrival of the Egyptian instructors."

The discussion now turned to the building of the city walls, and Mel directed a question to the Chief of the Elders. "Sirach, what has been achieved so far with this project?"

"Lord Melchizedek, there has been some progress, but it is very slow because we can only afford a small number of workers. Unless we can put more resources into this, I fear that the walls will never be completed."

"I understand," said Mel. "Up to now we have had little money to do this building work. Although our finances are improving, money will now have to be spent on our new army. I shall accept Pharaoh Mentuhotep's offer to supply some engineers and laborers to help with this project. When they arrive, we can again review the budget for this, to see how many of our own craftsmen we can employ to join them."

Sirach was pleased that more resources would be made available so that progress could be accelerated, but he was concerned that he would no longer be in charge of the project. Mel reassured him: "I will make it clear to the Egyptians that you have overall responsibility for this building work. They will report to you, and you will need to be satisfied with any suggestions that the engineers make, and ensure that there are no delays due to idleness or faulty workmanship. If our foreign guests cause any trouble, you must report it to me and I shall write to the Pharaoh about it. Finally, please consult with Chancellor Jacob to ensure that we do not run over budget."

"Thank you Sir," the Elder responded. "I shall do as you ask. You can be assured that this project will be well managed, and I am honored that you have put your trust in me."

All that remained was for Mel to ask Secretary Daniel to meet him the following morning, so that a reply to Pharaoh's message could be drafted. As there were no further comments or questions, he declared the meeting closed, and invited all present to enjoy another goblet of wine before they departed.

In his message to Mentuhotep, Mel assured the Pharaoh that he understood the reasons why troops could not be spared, but accepted with gratitude the offer of both military advisors and help with the wall building. He promised to give Egypt priority for all the exports it required, and welcomed the safe corridor for transportation. A similar passageway would be established between Salem and the port of Jaffa.

"It will take more than a full day to translate your message and prepare the parchment for your signature," said Daniel. "Hannu needs a short rest after his journey here, but then he will be able to take the document back to Egypt by the fastest route."

"Very well, Daniel," Mel replied. "Please continue to offer Hannu our hospitality until he is ready to leave, and supply him with what he needs for his journey. Bring him to me before he departs, so that I can wish him a safe trip. I shall arrange for two of our new military recruits to accompany him as far our own border." Two days later, the messenger left Salem for his home country.

Mel now resumed his governance routine that included holding court to hear legal cases, meeting with his inner cabinet members, and twice-weekly visits to the Temple. He also liked to make frequent tours of the city to assess for himself progress with various projects, and especially the wall building.

So far, he felt he had managed to fulfill the role of King and High Priest far more successfully than he could have imagined. There was just one worry: how would he cope if he also had to become a general and have to lead his troops into battle? He had no knowledge of warfare, and could only hope that the need for this would not arise. But would his "hope" serve to protect him from the harsh reality of life in Salem?

Several weeks went by before the assistance offered by Pharaoh eventually arrived in Salem. The financial situation continued to improve, buoyed by the increase in trade, especially with Egypt. The military advisors helped Lieutenant Baruch to train the fledgling army, and the wall building received a boost with the arrival of the engineers and laborers.

It was fortuitous that Salem was situated on a rocky plateau, as this in itself was an advantage when planning the city's defenses. The first action by the Egyptian builders was to organize the digging of a ditch around the outside of where the wall would be, once it had been completed. This would make it especially difficult for invaders to approach the walls with battering rams, or horse-drawn chariots.

To provide additional strength to the perimeter outer wall, especially at its most vulnerable sections, the engineers recommended constructing an inner section. The two would then be linked with cross-walls. These would create small rooms where troops could be stationed. Although this would add to the cost of the project, it was decided to accept this suggestion, subject to the money being available. However, priority must be given to completing the main wall first. [33]

Whilst on his patrols, Mel noted with satisfaction the progress with the building work, and he endorsed all the major decisions. Everything seemed to be going well in Salem, but he was at risk of becoming too relaxed and complacent. This feeling was rudely shattered when, late one evening, Lieutenant Baruch requested an urgent audience with him.

"Lord Melchizedek, our patrols have received word that a major attack on Salem is being planned. Sihon, the Amorite King, is forming an army from among the nomadic raiders that used to invade and rob us before our patrols were introduced. He is aware that our land has become more prosperous, and that there are riches to be seized if we can be defeated." [34] This was just the news that Mel had hoped he would never hear. "Sir," Baruch continued. "We shall have to mobilize our forces immediately, and you will have to lead them into battle to overcome the enemy before it has the chance to reach Salem."

Chapter 12

WARRIOR KING

M el tried to sound confident in his response to Baruch. "This is indeed of great concern, and we must take action as soon as we can. Please meet with me when the sun has risen tomorrow, and bring the Egyptian military advisers with you. We can then discuss our battle plan."

His lieutenant departed, and Mel retired to bed to try and collect his thoughts on this unwelcome news. Hopefully, an effective strategy could be agreed that would not place him in a position where his ignorance in such matters would be exposed, and his troops subjected to unnecessary risk. He had been told by Archangel Michael that he would receive guidance in the performance of his role in Salem, and he prayed to El Elyon that this would be given to him now.

Eventually he drifted off into a fitful sleep, and very soon experienced a dream that Michael was speaking to him. Or was he actually awake, and the Archangel was with him in the room? He was unable to tell, but the message he was hearing was certainly strong and clear. "Melchizedek, your prayer has been heard, and I have been sent to give you reassurance that you will know what to do when the time comes, and you will have the ability to carry it out." After a short pause, he continued, "The promise I gave you earlier will not be broken. El Elyon will be at your side. You will become a Warrior King." Mel was about to reply, but the image quickly faded, and he was once more alone.

Lieutenant Baruch arrived on time next morning, accompanied by two Egyptians. He introduced them as Intef, a General, and his assistant Meru who was also an official at Pharaoh's court. Fortunately, they both understood enough of the local language to be able to communicate without the constant need of translation. Mel first asked for a report on the current state of Salem's permanent army.

"Lord Melchizedek," began Baruch, "We have nearly one hundred full-time members of the force. I can also call on a similar number of volunteers who used to help with the patrols. Whilst we shall probably be outnumbered by the enemy, we will no doubt be better trained and organized than them."

"You have made excellent progress, Baruch," replied Mel. "Let us now hear from the Egyptians on the readiness of our troops to engage in live-action combat."

General Intef began to speak. "Sir, your men are already becoming skilled in the use of lance, sword, and bow. They are developing into a well-disciplined army, and should be a fighting force to be reckoned with. Up to present, they have successfully repelled raids by groups of marauding nomads, but have yet to engage in a major battle."

"I am very pleased to hear this," Mel said. "My concern is that King Sihon's army will be much larger than ours. Do you have some advice on tactics we could adopt that would give us an advantage?"

"Indeed we shall have several advantages, the first being one of surprise. Although Sihon will be prepared for us mounting a defense when he invades Salem, I doubt very much that he will be expecting us to take the initiative and attack his troops before he is ready."

Intef now made it obvious that he was addressing Mel personally. "Sir, I recommend that you lead your men stealthily toward the King's army during the night. Then, as soon as dawn breaks, charge forward and cut the enemy down."

Despite the assurances given by the Archangel during his nocturnal visit, Mel could not help but feel anything but trepidation at the thought of this vicious assault on fellow human beings. He did his best to conceal this sign of weakness, and said to Intef, "Have you any more suggestions?"

"Yes, Sir. Arrange the forces in a line, and place your archers at the left and right flanks. On your command, let them fire arrows and slingshots at the enemy, whilst everyone makes as much noise as possible. This surprise attack will create panic and confusion among Sihon's men. Then, on your command, lead those in the centre, armed with swords and spears, and bear down on those who remain, to finish the job." [35]

Mel liked these ideas, and he started to feel just a little more confident that he might just succeed in this mission. But Intef still had some further advice.

"You will probably find that many of the enemy will flee the camp, leaving everything behind. Do not chase after them. It may be a deliberate ploy to fragment our already small force, so that Sihon's soldiers can then re-form and overpower you. Once victory is complete, gather up anything useful that the defeated army has left behind—weapons, money, jewelry: they are the spoils of war, and they are yours. After this, the enemy will think carefully before daring to mount another invasion."

With that, all that remained was to agree on when to start the invasion. In order to maintain the element of surprise, there was no time to delay. They would need the remainder of the day to gather together the men, the equipment, and all the supplies they would need for the invasion. Only a few horses were available, so Mel, Baruch, and some of the other leaders would ride, and the remainder of the troops would be infantry. Tomorrow they would complete the preparations, and rest during the daylight hours. They would then set off as soon as it was dark.

Fortunately there was some moonlight when the modest army started its journey.

Baruch had arranged for three scouts to go ahead of them, to report back when they had located Sihon's camp. After eight hours of travelling eastwards, firstly past Salem's outlying farms, and then through the countryside, one of the scouts returned and said, "Sir, the enemy is about one kilometer from here. It all seems very quiet, and we have not yet seen any guards posted. My two colleagues are exploring the extent of the camp."

"Very good," said Mel. "Are we able to proceed further without being observed?"

"Yes Sir, if you are very quiet, you can move forward for over half a kilometer, and remain there undetected until you are ready to attack." On hearing this, they advanced as silently as possible until they reached a suitable spot behind a cluster of trees. They then arranged themselves into the battle formation that Intef had suggested. As dawn was still an hour away, there was an opportunity for a short rest and some final preparations.

As the time approached for the battle, Mel was starting to become nervous again. He knew he had to show that he was the supreme commander, and bravely lead the fighters, but he still had an aversion to personally slicing into people with a sword. It was thus with some relief that he learned something during a final, whispered briefing with Baruch and the other officers. Yes, he would initially lead the charge on horseback, but then fall back and allow the fighting men to overtake him and engage the enemy in the hand-to-hand combat. Those in command needed to be able to observe from the rear what was taking place in front of them, and then issue orders to the troops as required.

The night was coming to an end, and there was now sufficient light to see what they were doing. There was little sign of activity in the enemy camp, and no evidence yet that they had been seen. It was time to begin the encounter. The whole army slowly advanced, with everyone still being as quiet as they could, and halted when Sihon's camp was within range for the archers. Mel then gave the order for everyone to make a great noise by blowing trumpets, and banging swords on shields.

As the Egyptian advisers had anticipated, there was obvious panic in the camp, with men stumbling half awake out of their tents to see what was happening. During this confusion, the archers and sling-shottists let lose a hale of arrows and other missiles. Although there were some casualties, it looked like many of the enemy were running away. After the salvos appeared to have served their purpose, and to avoid the risk of casualties among his own infantry troops, Mel ordered a cease fire. With a great shout of encouragement, he then spurred his horse forward to lead the charge of the central unit of swordsmen. The terracotta-colored cloak he had decided to wear for the battle streamed out behind him as he galloped forward.

He dutifully held back just before reaching the camp, and his soldiers charged past, making a great commotion and attacking every enemy soldier they encountered. It was all over surprisingly quickly. Baruch went forward and consulted with some of his men. He then came to Mel and reported, "Sir, it appears that the enemy that has not been killed has fled, leaving all their possessions behind."

"Is there any sign of King Sihon?" Mel asked.

"No Sir. The royal tent is there, but the king has taken flight with his troops."

Mel's next question was, "Do you yet know the extent of the casualties on both sides?"

"We have suffered no deaths. Some of our men have been wounded, but none severely. There was little time for the enemy to grab their weapons and engage in serious hand-to-had combat." Baruch paused for a moment, and then continued, "As for Sihon's soldiers, we have so far found about twenty bodies. There are no wounded, so any that there were must have been helped to escape."

"This has been very successful, Baruch," replied Mel. "Let us do the decent thing and bury the bodies. Then ask the men to search the camp and collect everything of value they can find. This includes food, clothing, and weapons, as well as money, jewelry, and objects made of gold and silver. This will help to pay for our own forces.

They agreed to remain where they were for the rest of the day, and the night. This would enable them bury the dead, collect all the spoils of war, and then rest before returning to Salem. There was, however, also a strategic reason. It was possible that Sihon and his remaining army had not fled very far, and intended to return to their camp, either to salvage what remained of their possessions, or to counter-attack Mel's troops when they least expected it. Baruch posted guards at each outpost for the rest of their stay, to ensure that they would have adequate warning should this happen.

Although the guards reported that there may have been an occasional prowler who remained hidden, there was no attack. If Sihon returned now to collect his belongings, he would find precious little left for him. Once they had taken all that they needed, Mel's men made sure that what remained was put to the torch.

Early the next morning, the victors set off on their triumphant journey home, complete with their bounty. Two messengers were sent on ahead, unburdened by heavy equipment, to inform the inhabitants of Salem of their victory. The rest of the party arrived at the city just as the sun was setting, and were greeted by cheering crowds. They made their way to the Palace, where the valuables taken from Sihon's camp were deposited at the treasury; these would make a valuable contribution to the city's income. The troops then went off to their barracks, taking with them the confiscated weapons and other military items that would be useful.

It was clear that the crowd expected Mel to make a speech before going inside the Palace. He therefore summarized what had occurred, praised Baruch and the other officers for their leadership, and the men for their bravery and skill. His own contribution had been modest, and the engagement little more than a skirmish, but the crowd clearly wished to acknowledge him as their victorious leader. They repeatedly chanted, "Hale to Melchizedek, Warrior, King and High Priest. Thus, he had now achieved in the three roles he was expected to play in Salem. [36]

As he entered the building and out of sight of the crowds, Mel felt a sense of both joy and relief. Joy that, despite his doubts, he had succeeded; relief that this episode was now over. There would certainly be other battles to fight in the future, but the victory this time will have shown others who may contemplate invading Salem, that his men were quite capable of fighting back. It had been a memorable few days; he retired to his room to rest, giving thanks in his prayers to El Elyon.

———————

"Lord Melchizedek, an army has set up camp in the Kidron Valley just outside Salem." It was Obadiah, the chief servant. His voice was agitated—excited even, but did not display a sense of panic.

Mel first reaction was one of shock. "Are we about to be invaded? If so, we must quickly mobilize our own troops, and attack the aggressors."

"No Sir, it is most certainly not a threat. Like you, the leader of the army is a holy man, and also a Warrior King. He is returning home after defeating King Chedorlaomer, and liberating the city of Sodom."

Mel was relieved that he would not have to lead his own forces into battle again, at least not so soon after the last time. He asked, "Do we know the name of this successful leader?"

"Yes Sir," replied Obadiah. "His name is Abraham. He and his men are weary and hungry; they just want to rest for a while."

"Then I must go out and meet this man, and offer him some hospitality. Please ask your staff to prepare some food, and we shall take it out to Abraham and his army as soon as it is ready."

Whilst Obadiah was away organizing the refreshment, Mel gave careful thought to the meeting that would shortly take place. This would be his first encounter with somebody who was performing a similar role to his. Would they be equals, or should one defer to the other? Would there be a feeling of rivalry between them, or would they accept that they were kindred spirits, and servants of the same Lord?

When the food and drink were ready, Mel led Obadiah and a small group of junior servants out through the city gate and down into the valley. Below him, he could see a camp of about three hundred men. One tent was obviously larger and more embellished then the rest. He surmised that this must be where Abraham would be, and he guided the others toward it.

Just as he was arriving, two regal personages emerged. Judging from the animated conversation, there must have been some disagreement between them. One of the men then walked away, leaving his erstwhile companion standing alone at the entrance to the tent. Unsure of whom he was addressing, Mel approached and introduced himself. "Sir, I am Melchizedek, King of Salem. I have brought some food and drink for you and your men."

The other man immediately went down on one knee. "Your Lordship, I am your humble servant Abraham. It is indeed an honor to meet you, as I have heard stories of the coming of a King of Righteousness, who has the Badge of Priesthood on his breast."

Mel observed the bearded figure kneeling before him. He was still dressed as a warrior, and wearing some items of body amour, but his kingly appearance was enhanced by a richly-colored blue cloak and a golden helmet. "Bless you, Abraham," Mel replied. "I ask El Elyon to also bless you, and I thank him for giving you victory over your enemies. Let me offer you some bread and wine, and permit my servants take the rest of the refreshments to your weary troops."

At Mel's beckoning, Abraham stood up. "Thank you, Your Lordship, I am very grateful to accept this, and my men will be too. King Bera of Sodom, now free of the forces that occupied his city, has just asked me to accept the treasures captured during my campaign, by way of thanks for liberating him. Whilst I let my troops receive their share of what belongs to them, I have refused to take anything for myself." He concluded, "I do not want an earthly king like Bera to be able to say that he made me rich, but you are a messenger from El Elyon." [37]

The two men went into the tent, where Mel firstly administered the bread and wine to Abraham, and then had some himself. They chatted over the meal and realized that they were, in a way, distantly related. Abraham was a descendent of Noah's son, Shem, whilst Mel's earthly father, Nir, was Noah's brother. The other obvious thing they had in common was that they were both royal figures, and each had succeeded in the roles of both Priest and Warrior. There was, however, an important difference between them, as Abraham was shortly to point out.

Firstly, though, Abraham said, "As an acknowledgement of how El Elyon guided me to victory in my campaign, I shall give to you, his representative on earth, a tenth of all I have." Mel was not only surprised by this gesture, but also embarrassed. He knew that tithes were paid by subordinates to those in higher office, but he did not feel superior to Abraham. His first reaction was to decline this generous gift, but he realized that it might be an insult to do so. Thus, he humbly accepted it, knowing that it would help the city's finances and the work that still remained to be done.

Eventually it was time for the two men to depart. They embraced each other and then Abraham made his final observation, one that would keep replaying in Mel's mind for many years to come. "Lord Melchizedek," he said. "Whilst there are many similarities between us, there is one difference. "Whilst I am mortal, and will one day leave this earth, you will be a Priest of Priests for ever." [38]

Chapter 13

FEMALE COMPANY

With this important test of his ability to provide leadership in battle, as well as in domestic and spiritual matters, behind him, Mel felt that his apprenticeship must be complete. He was now entering a period of consolidation. Archangel Michael had been correct. Although he had been faced with many situations for which he considered himself ill prepared, somehow the promised guidance, knowledge and protection had all been made available to him. There was still much he did not understand, including the major question of why he personally had been chosen to fulfill the role into which he had been thrust.

The notion that he was an actor in some epic play kept recurring. There was something not quite real about his existence, almost as if he would suddenly wake up and find that it was all a dream. If this were the case, then the illusion had now continued for a long time, and had embraced many episodes. The dream, if that is what it was, was becoming the reality and what was there before it was now rapidly receding into a distant memory.

The weeks went by, and progress continued. Thanks to the increase in trade that the strengthened security had help to bring, plus the spoils of war and Abraham's tithes, Salem's finances were in a healthy state. The small but well-trained army was prepared for any threat of invasion, and it certainly looked like the city walls would eventually be completed. It would have been all too easy to slip into a state of complacency; those leaders who had fallen into this trap had given opponents a welcome opportunity to strike at them when their guard was down.

Mel maintained his program of regular audiences in the Palace throne room for his senior aids, Elders and also heard pleas from those who needed his advice and help. He offered prayers in the Temple, and often toured the city to see what was happening for himself. Although things were going well, there was something lacking in his life, and it took quite some time for him to identify just what it was.

Once again, it was a dream that made him realize what he was missing. As had happened in previous nocturnal episodes, he found himself floating above a very different habitat to that of Salem. He saw people going about their business, in and out of houses; up and down the shopping streets. Mel moved in closer, and searched among the faces. What was he looking for? Was there someone he might recognize down there? He did not know; it was an impulse he could not explain.

He relaxed his gaze, and started to feel a growing sense of melancholy. Then it came to him. He was sad because he was lonely. Whilst he met many people every day, men and women he could respect and trust, his elevated status meant that there was nobody he could regard as his equal—his friend. He needed a companion and, more specifically, a female companion. Up to now he had been too preoccupied with matters of state to think of this, but the desire had obviously been steadily growing until, now, it had burst through into his consciousness.

Mel recalled the first conversation he had had with the Chief Servant which, after all that had happened in the meantime, now seemed a long time ago. Obadiah had told him that he was sorry there were no concubines living in the Palace, but that he could arrange for some to call whenever Mel wished for it. He had not taken advantage of this offer at the time, finding the idea rather repulsive, and he had no intention of doing so now. It was, nevertheless, time to explore how he might end his present bachelor status, and seek a consort both for companionship and to support him in his royal duties. There was also the matter of who will be his heir, able to maintain the role that he had now established.

He would start by discussing this with Obadiah. During the time he had been in Salem, Mel had come to regard his Chief Servant as someone with whom he could discuss confidential matters, knowing that what was said would go no further. He was very unsure of his own age, as his physical development had occurred at a rate devoid of respect for normal chronology. Whilst his appearance might suggest he was a mature adult approaching middle age, his life experiences and mental acuity were commensurate with those of a much younger person. Knowing this, he valued the input of those who were older, and more worldly-wise than himself.

Obadiah was such a person, and he invariably dispensed useful advice when his views were sought. Mel came straight to the point, "You once asked me if I would like visits from concubines, but it is not my wish to avail myself of these women. Instead, I have been thinking about searching for a suitable lady who could become my queen."

He paused, to let the full impact of this statement register with his trusted servant. "Indeed, My Lord, I understand your need for a consort. If you left us for any reason, Salem would again be without a leader. We would anticipate that a married king would sire children who would be in line of succession, and thus we would have continuity.[39] I am sure that the people of Salem would rejoice at the prospect of a royal wedding."

"I am glad to hear this, Obadiah. No doubt there are many eligible women in the city who are commoners, but I wonder if there are some who are already of royal blood. It may be expected that I would marry a princess. This would avoid the jealousy that would occur among the citizens if I chose a bride from among their number." Mel was warming to his task, and continued, "Also, it would preserve the status of the monarchy, and may even have the advantage of forging a political alliance with a neighboring state that would encourage peaceful cooperation."

"Indeed, My Lord, this would certainly be an advantage for Salem. As you know, we are surrounded by small nations that have their own kings or chieftains. Whilst there may be those who would welcome closer ties with us, you have already seen that at least some of them will lose no opportunity to invade us. Thus," concluded Obadiah, "I find it difficult to recommend any potential escorts from among their number."

"This is unfortunate," commented Mel. "Do we have knowledge of any eligible women from other countries who could be approached?"

"Sir, you will recall the visit of nobleman Hannu, who delivered the response from Pharaoh Mentuhotep." Mel nodded, and encouraged Obadiah to continue. "Your Secretary, Daniel, became friendly with him during his brief stays with us. He learned that the Pharaoh has a daughter whom is unmarried. Perhaps you would like to ask Daniel to join us so he can relate what he knows about her."

The Secretary was duly sent for, and Mel briefly summarized the previous discussion. He then continued: "Daniel, Obadiah tells me that you have heard about Mentuhotep's daughter. Please, share with us what you know about her."

"Her name is Princess Aushead," began Daniel. "She has Nubian ancestry, and a dark, African skin. Hannu says she is very beautiful. Because the Pharaoh has sons who will succeed him, his daughter has no useful role to play in the royal court."

"This is very interesting to hear, Daniel. Did Hannu give any indication that she is seeking a suitor?"

"Although he did not specifically say this, many men who were commoners would be delighted to marry Aushead, but Egyptian Pharaohs are regarded as gods. Mentuhotep will not permit the royal blood to be mixed with that of the ordinary people." [40]

The more that Mel heard, the stronger became his belief that an ideal opportunity was presenting itself. It was one that would not only fulfill his own need for a consort, but it would also help with Salem's future peace and prosperity. In order to take this idea further, he understood that the correct protocol had to be followed. It was Daniel who pre-empted the question that he was about to be asked.

"Lord Melchizedek, if you wish to pursue this avenue, then I suggest that I compose on your behalf a letter to Pharaoh Mentuhotep. You would say that you have been told about his daughter, and her beauty, and that you would welcome the opportunity to meet her for yourself. It will be obvious to him what may result from this. If he does not approve of a potential future marriage between you and Aushead, then he will decline the request for an introductory meeting."

Mel liked what Daniel had advised. He said, "The letter should commence with my thanks for the trade pact, and the help of the military advisers, plus that of the wall builders. As the army has been trained and has proved its competence, I shall confirm with Lieutenant Baruch and the other leaders that they now feel confident to take full responsibility for the forces themselves. If they agree, then the advisers can return to Egypt and take the letter with them." Obadiah endorsed what had been said, and he and Daniel departed. Mel was left alone to muse on what it might be like if the meeting with the Egyptian Princess came to fruition.

The next morning Mel sent for Lieutenant Baruch and the two military advisors, Intef and Meru. "Gentlemen," he began. "We have had a successful military campaign, and the army now seems to be up to strength and fully trained." Addressing the two Egyptians, he said, "I would like to thank you both for the excellent way you have trained and advised our forces. Do you now think that your mission is complete, and that you can return to Egypt, confident that we can remain capable of defending ourselves?"

General Intef replied. "We have been happy working here, Lord Melchizedek, and we have been well looked after during our stay. Lieutenant Baruch has responded to our suggestions and proved to be an able commander. There is little more we can teach him, therefore we agree that this is an appropriate time for us to return to our home country."

"Very well," said Mel. "I shall promote Baruch to the rank of General, and we can ensure there is a competent chain of command from among those who served valiantly in the recent battle." This pronouncement appeared to have been well received, especially by the Lieutenant. He then added, "A letter is being prepared for your Pharaoh, and it will be ready in two days. You may then take your leave of us, but I ask that you carry the letter with you, and deliver it personally to Pharaoh Mentuhotep as soon as you reach Thebes."

This request was agreed, and the military advisers withdrew to make preparations for their return, using the safe passage that had been established for trade between the two countries. Daniel prepared the letter in his usual very correct and diplomatic style. Mel made sure that his interest in meeting Princess Aushead was clearly stated, and he then signed the scroll. Shortly thereafter, Intef and Meru bade their farewell to Salem, and were accompanied by an escort as far as the coastal city of Jaffa.

There was little Mel could do now but try not to be impatient whilst waiting for Pharaoh's reply. He devoted himself to his usual round of duties at the Palace and the Temple, ensuring that the business of the city continued to function safely and efficiently. There was just one niggle in his mind: was he being disloyal in seeking a relationship with this Egyptian Princess? But why should he be? There was no other woman in his life—or was there? Rational thought told him that he had no close contact with any woman in Salem; his deepest intuition hinted that he had already promised himself to another.

No matter how hard he concentrated, he could not resolve this dichotomy. What he was sure of, however, was that he did not want to continue indefinitely in his present bachelor state. For his own satisfaction, and for the good of Salem, he needed a wife and children. One day he would leave this land and, as Obadiah had pointed out, it was important that he had descendents to maintain continuity of the royal line.

The weeks seemed to pass slowly. Then the day came when Daniel announced that the messenger had arrived from Egypt.

It was the familiar figure of Hannu, who had been the courier of Pharaoh's first message, in what now seemed a long time ago. Mel ushered them both into his private room, eager to hear what the reply contained.

As before, his Secretary carefully translated from the scroll, consulting Hannu when he was unsure. "Pharaoh Mentuhotep sends his greetings, and is pleased with the advances made in Salem. His military advisers have told him about the development of the army, and the successes it has had in its campaigns." Yes, yes, all this is very courteous, thought Mel, but he was eager to hear if there was any word about the Princess. Nevertheless, he did not interrupt Daniel, but tried to maintain a calm, attentive listening expression as befitted his royal status.

And then it came. Daniel continued, "The Pharaoh would be happy for you to meet his daughter, Aushead, and suggests that he arranges for her to travel to Jaffa by royal barge. You will then be able to go on board and see her. There will be space on the vessel for you to remain there for several days if you wish. Other attendants from the court will be present, but Mentuhotep will have to remain in Thebes to guard against any attempt to usurp the throne during his absence."

Mel was delighted with this positive response, and wished to make the necessary arrangements without delay. Firstly he must send a reply to Pharaoh Mentuhotep. He immediately dictated a letter commencing with the usual pleasantries, and continuing with his acceptance of the suggested plan for meeting the Princess. Whilst he was now eager to get things moving, it would take time for his reply to be delivered, and even longer before all the arrangements could be made. Once again he would just have to be patient.

Although there were still matters of state to attend to, Mel's thoughts were now dominated by the forthcoming meeting. He had to tell himself to put emotion aside for the moment, and look at the situation rationally. When two royal persons from different countries meet in this way, there must be a protocol to ensure that appropriate diplomacy is preserved. Soon after Hannu had departed with the message for Pharaoh, he again summoned Obadiah and Daniel to discuss plans for what must now be referred to as a state visit.

After covering the preliminaries, such as the initial courtesies and an exchange of gifts, Mel jumped straight to the topic that was uppermost in his mind. "Gentlemen," he began, "Whether it is explicit or not, the main purpose of this meeting is to explore the possibility of a marriage between the Princess and me. If I wish to take Aushead as my wife, and she agrees, do you know what procedure has to be followed?"

It was Obadiah who responded first. "Sir, during my many years serving in the Palace, I have been present when several of your predecessors have married, although this has usually been to a local commoner. The King pays a "bride-price" to the girl's parents, and receives a gift in return. There is then a wedding ceremony, followed by a feast, and then the new wife enters her husband's house."

So far, this did not seem to create any problems, but it was Daniel's turn to speak. "My Lord, from talking to Hannu and others who have visited us, I understand that there is no wedding ceremony in Egypt. Instead, a marriage settlement is drawn up by the parents of both parties, and signed by witnesses." Anticipating Mel's question, he added, "If the parents are no longer available, as is the case with yourself, then the marriage partner personally signs the agreement. Then, as is the case in Salem, gifts are exchanged, and the woman is considered to be married when she enters her husband's house." [41; 42]

"Thank you both," Mel replied. "These customs do not create any difficulty except that, should Aushead and I wish to marry, it will take yet more time for messages to be exchanged with the Pharaoh, and agreements to be signed."

Daniel responded in a way that Mel had not foreseen. "Sir, as I mentioned when we first discussed sending the letter, Mentuhotep will have anticipated the reason for your wish to meet his daughter. He is probably happy to find a suitable suitor for her, and he may even have already drafted a settlement document. If so, this will be carried by a court official who will be present on the barge with the Princess."

"Are you confident of this, Daniel?" Mel asked, whilst trying to disguise his pleasure at hearing how the process could be foreshortened.

"Whilst I cannot be certain, Sir, it is reasonable to think that the Pharaoh will have no more desire for a protracted engagement than you have."

"Then we shall make the necessary arrangements from this end, and be ready to set off for Jaffa as soon as we have word that the royal barge is nearing the port." With that, the meeting came to a close.

Mel lost no time in planning for the journey, and what might result from it. He would leave General Baruch in charge during his absence, because maintaining law and order was the top priority. As gifts for Pharaoh Mentuhotep, he would take a generous quantity of the purple murex dye so beloved of the Egyptians, and some choice treasures that had been looted from the camp of the defeated King Sihon. Secretary Daniel would accompany him, as he would be able to translate conversations and documents if required. They would have an escort of six junior officers and men from the army.

All they had to do now was wait. The message finally arrived. The royal barge would be at Jaffa in three days time.

Chapter 14

THE PRINCESS

Early the following day the party of eight set off on horseback for the sixty-five kilometer journey to Jaffa. If they had rushed, they could have completed the trip before nightfall, but they decided to take a more leisurely two days over it and not subject their steeds to unnecessary strain. Their plan was to set up camp near the port, and then watch the arrival of the royal barge from there.

Mel had not visited this coastal town before, so he was looking forward to seeing how it fulfilled its key role as a staging post in international trade. The harbor was set in the middle of the gentle curve of a bay. Reaching out into the sea was a jetty that provided a safe mooring for the boats. Several cargo vessels were already docked there, and all manner of boxes, bales, and baskets were being off-loaded onto hand-carts or horse-drawn wagons.

Small fishing boats were pulled right up onto the beach, their nets hanging from the masts to dry in the warm sunshine. Set back from the shoreline was a mixture of warehouses, offices and clusters of cottages, plus a more impressive building that Mel suspected might be a temple. He immediately took a liking to Jaffa, and he could not fail to admire the efficient way that everyone seemed to be going about their business.

They decided to set up camp on a hill overlooking the sea, a short distance away from the other buildings. The next morning they would be able to watch for the arrival of the royal barge, and allow themselves time to descend to the harbor and be there by the time it docked. Once the tents had been erected, and the evening meal prepared and eaten, there was little to do but try to obtain some rest. Mel now started to feel excitement at the thought of meeting a beautiful princess the next day, but he was also nervous. Like many things that had happened during the last year or two, this would be a new experience for him. Would he say and do the right thing? Would he make a fool of himself? Or would he be guided by a force he still did not understand, as had been the case up to this point. Mercifully, sleep saved him from further mental anguish.

As the sun was rising, heralding a new day, the party partook their customary breakfast of fruit and nuts. Mel then positioned himself on the hillside, and looked westwards out to sea. He saw several fishing boats returning with their catches, and a few larger vessels that he assumed were freighters, but there was no sign of anything that could be the royal barge. But he was being impatient again. Sailing ships could not estimate their arrival time to the minute; journeys would depend on factors such as the strength of the wind, and the sea conditions.

The morning wore on, and it was time for the mid-day meal. Mel reluctantly dragged himself away from his vigil and, although his anxiety had curbed his desire for food, he managed to eat something. Before returning to his look-out position, he changed into his finest kingly robes so that he would look his most regal when the meeting took place—if it ever did! He had almost completed his clothing change when he heard an excited shout from the junior officer who had taken his place on the hillside.

"Sir, Sir, I can see something on the horizon that could be the royal barge." Mel rushed to the spot and looked to where the officer was pointing. Shielding his eyes, he saw a ship coming toward them that was certainly different from the others in Jaffa. It was glinting like gold in the afternoon sun, which had now passed its noon zenith and was starting to descend. As the vessel drew closer, he could see a single, large white sail emblazoned with the image of a crimson radiating orb. But that was not its only means of propulsion; on either side there were fifteen oarsmen, rowing in unison to the sound of a beating drum.

Mel announced that it was time for him to go down to the harbor, accompanied by Daniel and two of the military escort. They would carry with them the gift offerings they had brought for the Pharaoh. The other four soldiers would remain on the hillside to guard the camp.

They reached the jetty just as the barge was preparing to dock. It was indeed a sight to behold, with its hull covered in gold embellished with black bands that stretched all the way around the vessel. The prow and the stern were curled upwards, each topped with a carving of a mythical creature. Standing proud on the deck like little houses were three ornate cabins. The most elaborate one was positioned in the centre, which Mel assumed was for the royal princess. [43]

The arrival of such an impressive craft had drawn quite a gathering of on-lookers, keen to see who or what was being transported. It was fortunate that Mel had brought the two soldiers along, as they helped to keep the crowd back and allowed him to remain unhindered at the front. As the barge was being secured, he could see that there was also a military presence on board to provide protection for both the valuable vessel and its royal passenger.

As the gang plank was being lowered, a figure came to the side of the boat and started to speak. Mel was delighted to see that it was the nobleman Hannu; how thoughtful of the Pharaoh to include him in the party, knowing that he would be a familiar person to us. "Lord Melchizedek," he said, "Please come aboard and bring Daniel and your escort with you." This was the moment he had been waiting for, and they stepped onto the barge.

Once on deck, Hannu exchanged greetings with them, and asked for the gangplank to be raised so that nobody else would be tempted to climb on board. "Princess Aushead is looking forward to meeting you. I have been teaching her some of your language so that we shall not need to translate everything. Are you ready to enter the royal chamber now?" Mel confirmed that indeed he was, and they were ushered into the ornate central cabin.

The Princess was seated on an elaborately-carved, gilded chair, and there was a hand-maiden in attendance. Daniel respectfully held back and left Mel to move forward on his own. He bowed low and said, "Princess Aushead, I have been looking forward to meeting you."

She arose from her seat. "Lord Melchizedek, news of your impressive exploits in Salem has reached us. I too have been awaiting the opportunity for us to meet." The comments Mel had heard about the Princess's beauty had not been exaggerated. Her dark skin contrasted beautifully with the white robe she was wearing. The garment was held in place at the waist by a striped blue and gold belt, secured by a lapis lazuli broach. Around her shoulder-length black hair was a gold band studied with jewels of different colors and, at its centre, was the raised head of the sacred Egyptian cobra.

It was Mel's turn to speak again. "Your Highness, I have brought gifts of murex dye and treasures from our campaigns for your father; I hope you will accept them on his behalf."

"Thank you, Your Lordship; I am very pleased to receive them. Let me now show you around the royal barge. It will then be time for our evening meal, and I would be happy if you and Secretary Daniel could join me for this. Your two military escorts can dine with our own officers." Mel was certainly happy to agree; so far it was all going well, and he only hoped that it would continue in this way.

The barge was nearly fifty meters long. Whilst the top deck was richly embellished, the accommodation below for the sixty crew members, soldiers and other servants was plain but functional. Food was stored and prepared in a well-equipped galley. The visitors were impressed with the order and efficiency of what they saw, and it indicated to them just how advanced the Egyptians were in boat building and design.

When the time came for the evening meal, the Princess, her maid, Hannu, Mel, Daniel, and the ship's captain sat around a table set on the deck. They were hidden from the inquisitive eyes of those on shore by curtains that had been erected on either side. This was no ordinary fare—it was a royal banquet! The dishes came one after the other. There was wild fowl and locally caught fish, each accompanied by bread, beans, lentils, onions, leeks, and garlic. For desert there were grapes, figs, and dates. To drink there was beer and a range of fine Egyptian wines.

As the liquor took its effect, Mel started to relax for the first time since his leisurely days in the Garden of Eden. What started as a formal meal soon developed into a convivial party that continued late into the evening. When they could eat and drink no more, Princess Aushead said to him, "Sir, there is accommodation for you and Daniel in the forward cabin, and you would be welcome to spend the night on board." Mel was delighted to accept, especially as he had no wish to make his way back to the camp at this hour.

"I am very pleased you will be staying on board a while longer," she replied. "Tomorrow morning we can set off in the barge and take a trip to explore the coastline." He took this to be a strong indication that the Princess was keen to spend more time with him. If this were indeed the case, he could have no objections as he was already starting to enjoy her company. This would be a good opportunity to get to know her better.

Next morning they were served bread, honey and fruit, before emerging on to the deck to watch the preparations for their departure. The thirty oarsmen took their places and the ship was untied. When the captain gave the command, they rowed away from the jetty and out into the clear water. The vessel then headed out to sea, and the helmsman at the large steering oar set a northwards course. Now the drumbeats started to set the rhythm for the rowers. Mel had heard this sound the previous day as the barge approached Jaffa but, now that he was actually on board, the continuous pounding was irritatingly loud and made conversation difficult. Thankfully, relief was soon to come. The captain announced that there was now a favorable wind; the large sail could be raised and the oarsmen rested.

Now, in the blissful quietness, Mel could once again talk with the Princess. "This trip is very enjoyable, thank you for arranging it. Shall we be back in Jaffa in time for the evening meal?"

Aushead's reply came as a big surprise to him. "We shall go as far as the port of Tyre in Lebanon, and will arrive about mid-day tomorrow. The people there are friendly toward Egypt, and they will let us take on fresh water and fruit. After anchoring overnight, we can set off back to Jaffa the following morning."

It was quite obvious that the Princess had been deliberately devious, committing Mel to at least a three-day journey without going into detail about the "trip to explore the coastline." His initial reaction was that he should be angry at being manipulated like this, but he had to admit that, had she been more specific, he would still have readily agreed to the cruise. He welcomed the chance to be close to Aushead for three or four days, in such a relaxing environment and away from the crowds. Setting up this little ploy suggested to him that her feelings must be similar to his.

The voyage proceeded without incident, and Mel had to acknowledge that he was becoming very fond of the Princess. She was not only beautiful, but also intelligent and with a good sense of fun. Despite what may superficially have seemed to be just a diplomatic, goodwill meeting between royal personages of two countries, he had not lost sight of the real reason behind this encounter. He suspected that this was also the case with Aushead. During the final afternoon of the cruise, as the ship was only a few kilometers from Jaffa, he made up his mind to approach the matter head-on.

He found the Princess standing by herself on deck, gazing wistfully out to sea. Mel moved close to her. "What do you see, Aushead?" he asked.

"I am looking into the future," she responded ambiguously. When pressed to be more specific, she explained, "Soon this visit will be over, and I will return to Thebes to be with my father. This visit has been one of the happiest times I can remember."

Mel was still not sure if his royal visitor was being coyly suggestive, but he had already decided what to say. "Princess Aushead, it would be an honor if you would agree to be my wife, and Queen of Salem. I cannot promise you the same rich life-style you have enjoyed up to now, but I shall love and care for you with all my heart."

How would she respond? A second of time seemed like an hour. "Lord Melchizedek, I would like very much to be your wife and Queen, and devote my life to serving you and your kingdom."

Mel felt joy surge through his body; his life would now be complete. Up to now, royal protocol had inhibited all but superficial physical contact between them, but now this was swept aside. He took Aushead in his arms, and they held each other in an uninhibited, passionate embrace.

Daniel and Hannu were sent for and told of the decision. Whilst both expressed pleasure, and tried to sound as if the news was unexpected, they were nevertheless prepared for it and the formalities that would now be needed. "We need a marriage settlement drawing up," said Mel. "How long do you think it will take before a wedding ceremony can be arranged?"

Daniel answered on behalf of both of them. "Sir, in anticipation of the decision of you and the Princess, Pharaoh Mentuhotep has already supplied Hannu with a draft document. We now have to complete this ourselves, and it can then be immediately taken back to Thebes when the barge returns."

"Will the Princess have to return to Egypt, and then make the journey back to Salem when the settlement has been signed by her father?" Mel asked.

"No Sir, if you both wish, she can travel back to our city with us after we have docked in Jaffa. She will then take up residence with her maid in the Palace, in a room of her own. The wedding ceremony will take a little time to arrange, and we must allow Pharaoh the opportunity to notify us of any objections or conditions he may have. When the two of you are married, you will be able to live together as husband and wife."

This was all very efficient, as Mel had come to expect from his Secretary. "Thank you Daniel and Hannu, you have been most helpful. I shall tell the Princess that she can bring her hand-maiden to Salem with her. As soon as we arrive at Jaffa, I shall command one of our soldiers to go straight to Salem to inform General Baruch of these developments, and to ask Obadiah to prepare a private room for Aushead and her maid."

As it was late in the afternoon, they decided to remain on board until the next morning. This would give the scribes time to complete the marriage settlement, and also allow Aushead and her maid to pack up all their belongings. At daybreak, Mel sent one of his two soldiers back to Salem to convey the joyful news, and the other into the town to hire a horse-drawn carriage for the women and their possessions. The rest of his military escort would be asked to descend to the key side, and be ready to accompany the royal party back home.

With the document now completed and signed, and entrusted to Hannu for safe delivery to the Pharaoh, they bade farewell to him and the captain, and disembarked. Without any further delay, the barge pulled away from the jetty and set a course for Alexandria, taking with it the gifts of murex dye and the precious objects for Pharaoh Mentuhotep.

They again decided to take two days for their return to Salem. This would avoid unnecessary effort by the horses pulling the carriage along the sometimes rough tracks, and allow more time for the women's room to be prepared at the Palace. As the entourage approached the city, crowds came out to greet them, cheering and waving flags. Mel was grateful that the Princess was being welcomed so enthusiastically, and they both waved back in acknowledgement. It reminded him of his own entry to the city, which now felt to have taken place a long time ago.

They turned into the Palace yard, and were greeted by the sight of General Baruch heading a guard of honor that lined the drive that led to the front entrance. To compliment this, Obadiah had assembled all his staff and positioned them on either side of the doorway. The carriage came to a halt. Baruch stepped forward and announced: "Lord Melchizedek, may I welcome you home. Princess Aushead, I am your humble servant; it is a great joy that you are to join us here in Salem."

After thanking the General for his kind words, they alighted from the coach and entered the Palace, pausing only to exchange greetings with Obadiah. Once inside, Mel suggested that the Princess and her maid be immediately shown to their quarters. He then spent a few minutes conferring with Baruch on events that had occurred in his absence, and summarizing for him the current situation regarding his forthcoming marriage.

Sometime later, the royal couple was joined by the senior staff for the evening meal, but Mel was not sorry when the time came when he could retire to his room for some much needed rest. As he was drifting off into unconscious, his thoughts were invaded by doubts concerning the decision he had made. Was there some reason why he should not marry the Princess? Not for the first time, he wondered if he had already committed himself to another? Surely his mind was just playing tricks again; but perhaps . . . . . Sleep saved him from any further mental torment.

Chapter 15

THE PROCLAMATION

Princess Aushead was quick to settle comfortably into life at Salem. Mel took her with him on his tours of the city and his visits to the Temple. Wherever they went there were enthusiastic waves from the people, and the Princess was always ready to return the greeting with a cheery smile. It appeared that she was being well accepted by all those who saw her.

Despite his new-found happiness, Mel could not afford to neglect matters of state. Issues requiring decisions were still raised at his regular court sessions, and legal cases continued to be brought before him for judgment. Also, he did not wish to ignore the group of Elders, and the valued contributions they continued to make, especially in the commercial life of Salem. In preparation for his next meeting with them, he needed to ask Chancellor Jacob for a review of Salem's financial situation.

"Lord Melchizedek, you will recall that, when you first joined us, we did not have sufficient money to pay the palace staff their full wages. The lack of security in our city discouraged travelers stopping here to replenish their supplies. Business people were reluctant to trade with us for fear of being robbed. Our own citizens also suffered at the hands of invaders."

"Yes, I do remember that," replied Mel. "But then the situation started to improve when we first introduced the volunteer security patrols."

"Indeed it did, Sir. Visitors now feel safe calling here to buy their provisions from us. Then the trade agreement with Egypt boosted our exports, with the result that the income from tithes and taxes increased. Finally, both the bounty looted from your successful campaign against King Sihon and the gifts from Lord Abraham added considerably to our wealth."

Mel was reassured by this. "So, Jacob, are you quite satisfied that now we have sufficient revenue to sustain our present expenditure for the foreseeable future?"

The reply came as something of a shock. "No Sir, up to now the spoils of war and the gifts have enabled us to maintain our full-time army, and allowed the wall building to proceed at a brisk rate. Unfortunately, most of the looted treasures have now been sold. We shall shortly be reliant only on income from trade, tithes, and taxes to cover our costs, and it will not be enough to maintain our current spending."

"It is well that I know this," said Mel. "Have you any suggestions on how we can balance the books, and avoid overspending?"

"Sir, the economics are not complicated. We need to find a way either to increase our income, or reduce our outgoings, or both. Options for generating more money include raising taxes, increasing exports, finding a new source of revenue, or looting from another sovereign state. Your predecessor was faced with a similar situation, and he took the latter option. He went off with the army to conquer another country, and we never saw him again."

"Indeed, I do not want to make the same mistake," commented Mel. "Please investigate in more detail all the other ideas you have for increasing the city's income, and prepare a report for me. In the meantime, I shall meet with some of our leaders to discuss with them ways to cut down on our expenditure." Jacob expressed his agreement, and then departed to make a start on his assignment.

Mel then sent for Chief Elder, Sirach, and General Baruch. "Gentlemen, we have financial challenges facing us; very soon we shall not be able to maintain our current level of spending. Chancellor Jacob is investigating possible ways to raise more money, but the purpose of our meeting now is to agree on how we can cut costs"

It was Sirach who spoke first. Right from their first encounter he had been concerned about the need to complete the building of the city walls, and Mel had given him overall responsibility for overseeing the project. It was now time for a progress report.

"Sir, with the help of the Egyptians, the defensive ditch was finished some time ago, and we are very close to linking up the new section of wall with the old. It will soon be obvious to any potential invader that we are now a fully walled city. However, we know that we shall still be vulnerable if a battering ram is used. You will remember that the Egyptian engineers recommended constructing inner sections of the wall in certain places, with cross-linkages to add extra strength to the outer section."

"Yes, I do recall that, "Mel replied. "But the ditch was constructed for the very purpose of making it difficult for any wheeled machine of war to reach the ramparts. Because of our financial constraints, we may have to give a low priority to building the reinforcing layers. My question to you is, do we still need the Egyptians to help us? We are paying for their services so, if they can be spared, we shall be saving money."

The Chief Elder considered this carefully before he responded. "My Lord, in view of what you say, there should be no need to retain either the engineers or laborers any longer. Our own men will be able to complete the last stage of the outer wall, even though it will take longer to do. After that, even their services can be dispensed with if you wish."

"Very well, Sirach, in two or three week's time we are expecting a messenger to arrive from Egypt with the marriage document from Pharaoh Mentuhotep. You can tell all the Egyptian workers that, when the visitor returns home, they can travel back with him. But I wish to avoid hardship for our own men for as long as possible. Let them continue under your supervision. Repairs and maintenance will surely be needed on the completed wall. If they have the time, they can even make a start on the reinforcing structure."

It was now Baruch's turn to be questioned. "General, how many full-time soldiers do we now have?"

"Sir, we have one hundred and twenty men," was the reply. "But we can call on many more volunteers if we need to, just as we did for the last campaign."

Mel did not wish to emasculate the force to such an extent that it would be ineffective during an invasion, but he also needed the cost of maintaining it to remain within a realistic budget. "The army's earlier success will live long in the history of Salem," he said. "Would it be practical to reduce number of professionals, and increase the size of the volunteer force that would only be paid if and when they are needed in action?"

"As you know," the General replied. "The army has now taken over the role of the earlier neighborhood security patrols, and I would not want to have less than one hundred permanent soldiers. We can, if you wish, introduce a conscription scheme that requires all other able-bodied men to undergo basic military training, for which they would be paid. Then, if circumstances demand it, they can be called upon to supplement the regular force."

"An excellent idea," said Mel. "Please go now and take the necessary action. It is likely that this will generate at least some cost saving. I shall issue the decree that will make it mandatory for those eligible to undertake their military training." With that, the meeting ended. Although Mel would continually review the financial situation with Jacob, he was confident that good progress had been made toward achieving a balanced budget.

The task of closely monitoring the city's finances provided Mel with a much-needed diversion from being preoccupied with his forthcoming marriage to Aushead. It was not that he had doubts of it being a happy union, and one that would hopefully result in the establishment of a line of succession for the royal household. It was just that he could not shake off the feeling that sometime, somewhere, he was being disloyal to another woman. However, any uncertainty that may have been lingering at the back of his mind was put quickly aside by the announcement that Pharaoh's messenger had arrived.

Mel asked Daniel to immediately usher the visitor into the private meeting room, and he then called Aushead to join them. He was delighted to see that, once again, it was the familiar figure of nobleman Hannu. "May I welcome you back to Salem. Your journey has been quicker than I had expected."

"Indeed Sir, favorable winds on the voyage and the safe corridor from Jaffa have each served to reduce the travel time. I have brought for you the marriage certificate, now completed by Pharaoh Mentuhotep and, for the Princess, there are wedding gifts of fine linen cloth and a necklace of gold inlaid with jewels."

Mel was keen to hear what had been written in the document, and asked for a translation. Daniel spent a few moments scrutinizing the papyrus, and checking details with Hannu as necessary. "Sir, it is little changed from that which we completed whilst on the royal barge. The Pharaoh thanks you for your gifts, and grants permission for his daughter to marry you." Although this had been anticipated, Aushead's eyes sparkled with joy when she heard there were no last-minute stumbling blocks that could jeopardize their forthcoming marriage.

Daniel continued, "The Pharaoh again regrets that, for reasons of security, he will be unable to personally attend the wedding, but he has appointed nobleman Hannu to be his representative at the ceremony."

"This is all very good news," said Mel. "Let the preparations for the wedding ceremony and feast begin, so that we can cement the alliance between our two countries without delay."

Despite all the enthusiasm, the sobering influence of Salem's financial situation had to be considered. Instead of the lavish party envisaged for hundreds of people, with no expense spared for food and drink, a smaller affair would have to suffice. Mel consulted with Obadiah and Daniel to compile a guest list of no more than fifty individuals.

This would be based largely on seniority, but would include men and women who had made significant contributions to the life of the city. Among this number were members of the army who had distinguished themselves in battle, and the Elders who had achieved a high level of exports. There was one additional guest he wished to include: Benjamin, the farmer who had been so helpful when he was making his way to Salem for the very first time. The wedding date was set for two weeks hence.

There was now much to do. Mel could not neglect his stately and priestly duties in order to spend all his time preparing for his nuptials, but he did arrange a meeting with Princess Aushead, Daniel and Hannu to plan the format of the ceremony itself.

They agreed that it would be held during the afternoon, to allow time in the morning for dealing with any urgent business, before attending to personal grooming and dressing for the wedding. Neither Mel nor his betrothed would commission special wedding clothes, preferring instead to rely on their royal robes to provide the necessary pageantry for this special occasion.

Nobleman Hannu then spoke. "Once the guests have assembled, and the appointed time has arrived, the people will stand and the bride and groom will enter the room together. I shall then announce: 'We are here to celebrate the wedding of Melchizedek, King and High Priest of Salem, and Princess Aushead of Egypt. I am authorized by Pharaoh Mentuhotep to give his daughter in marriage to your King.'"

Daniel was next to contribute. "During other weddings I have attended, it was usual for a priest to ask for a divine blessing on the union, but the only such official that we have now is yourself, the one who is to be married."

Mel thought for a moment and then said, "I shall ask the people to repeat after me this prayer to El Elyon: 'God in heaven, I ask you to bless this marriage between Princess Aushead and King Melchizedek. May it be long and happy, and produce many descendents who can continue to proclaim you as the one true Lord.'"

His knowledgeable Secretary spoke again. "The next step will be for each of you to publically proclaim your commitment to each other, and to the sanctity of matrimony." Addressing Mel, he continued, "Sir, it will be expected that you will then place a veil over the Princess's face, and loudly announce: 'She is my wife.' After that, her maid will hand you a small phial of the finest perfume, and you will pour it over your wife's head. The final act will be for the two of you to exchange gold rings and place them each other's fingers."

Aushead had been listening silently to all this, and she now spoke. "Thank you Hannu and Daniel for explaining what will happen. Will the placing of the rings mark the end of the ceremony?"

"Yes Your Highness," Daniel answered. "We can then expect the guests to loudly applaud and cheer you both, acknowledging that you are now husband and wife. You may then take your places at the top table to enjoy the feast."

As there were no further questions, and everyone appeared to be clear what would happen, the meeting closed and each went to attend to their respective duties.

Over the next few days, Mel started to wonder how the wedding day would be perceived by the wider population of Salem. Although he and his future wife had been welcomed by enthusiastic crowds when they arrived from Jaffa, only a small number of them would be present at the ceremony. Because the occasion was not going to be the over-indulgent and costly affair that it might have been, had there been no budget constraints, he began to think how it could be linked to something else that would be forever remembered. An idea started to take shape in his mind, and it eventually developed into a firm resolve. He would make a proclamation during the wedding ceremony.

Firstly, though, as was his practice, he needed to discuss this with those he could trust. Chief Elder, Sirach, and Chancellor Jacob would each be affected in some way by what he was about to propose, so they would be the ideal confidants.

"Gentlemen," Mel began. "In celebration of my marriage to Princess Aushead, I have decided to proclaim this year a 'Jubilee

Year', the start of which will be indicated by a long blast on a ram's horn trumpet." He paused, leaving his two guests to wonder just what this would mean. "This will be a time when all debts will be cancelled, and all property will be returned to its rightful owners. In addition, those who are slaves, or are unfairly tied by contracts to serve their masters, shall be set free." [44]

Before waiting to hear the reaction to this, he added, "It shall be written into the Statute Book that there will be in my name a Jubilee Year every fifty years, and the same conditions will apply. This will prevent injustices continuing indefinitely, and give hope to those who suffer at the hands of the rich and powerful."

It was some time before anyone spoke. Then Sirach broke the silence. "Sir, we must respect your wishes, but many of my business associates rely on indentured labor to remain profitable. How will they be able to continue if all their employees leave them?"

Mel's reply left the Chief Elder feeling rather shameful. "If the worker has been treated fairly and paid what is due, then he or she will not want to leave their employer even though they are free to do so. Only those who have been exploited and underpaid will want to seek work elsewhere."

It was Jacob's turn to wonder if Mel's idea was realistic. "Some of our wealthy citizens provide a useful service by lending money to those who need it. They also contribute to the Treasury by paying taxes on the profits they make from this."

Again the response may not have been what the Chancellor wished to hear.

"Money lenders who are honest, who do not charge exorbitant interest, and who only loan sums that they know their clients can repay, will surely remain in business. But those who cause hardships and despair by lending unrealistic amounts at a high premium, deserve to lose their money."

Sirach and Jacob found it difficult to disagree with these arguments and, after some further discussion, they expressed their approval that the proclamation would be announced at the wedding feast.

Mel allowed himself a feeling of satisfaction that this idea had come to him—or was it a divine intervention?— and that the proclamation would be take place. He felt that, whatever successes and failures the future might hold for him, the Jubilee Year would be his lasting legacy.

There were still duties to attend to, and final preparations to be made, but soon the eve of the wedding was upon them. Mel retired to bed early, determined to enjoy a good night's rest—it would be the last time he would be alone in this room. He tried to sleep but, once again, the feeling that something was amiss invaded his mind. Was he doing the right thing in marrying Princess Aushead? Was he being disloyal by doing so? The answers did not come but, eventually, sleep did, saving him from further soul-searching.

Chapter 16

THE DECISION

The telephone rang. It took a few moments for Mel to realize the significance of this. A telephone—in ancient Salem? Perhaps he had just been dreaming again. He opened his eyes and waited until they had adjusted to the glare of the sun that was streaming into the room through a gap in the curtains. Sure enough, there on his bedside table was a telephone, and it was still ringing. Only then did he realize that he was no longer a king living four thousand years ago, but was back in the twenty-first century. He picked up the handset and announced himself. It was his fiancée, Angelina.

"I know it's Sunday morning," she said. "But are you still in bed, you lazy devil? All that wine you drank during the dinner last night must have really knocked you out!" Mel glanced at his watch on the bedside table, and saw that it was just after ten o'clock in the morning. Despite the pleasure of hearing the cheerful voice of the girl he was to marry, Mel was keen to complete the call quickly, so that he could try to take stock of his situation.

"Don't forget that we are meeting my mum and dad here at twelve o'clock, so that we can finalize our wedding plans. They promised to treat us to a pub lunch afterwards."

"How could I forget such an important appointment," Mel replied, more than a little untruthfully in view of his current mental turmoil. "See you at noon. Love you." With that, he replaced the handset and attempted to reconcile all the thoughts and emotions that were spinning around in his head.

If he had just had a dream about a past life, it had been a very detailed one, and he could recall sufficient features of it to enable him write a book. He had gone right back in history, firstly spending time with Noah and his family. Then somehow he had been transported to the Garden of Eden, where he had spent a year camping out in that idyllic place. When this had come to an end, he had been spirited to the ancient city of Jerusalem, which at that time was called Salem. Apparently, he had displayed a bodily characteristic that identified him as a King and High Priest. Once appointed, he had fulfilled his obligations competently, and had even fought a successful battle.

Mel thought for a moment, trying to remember what came next. Ah yes, how could he forget; it involved a lady whom apparently he wanted to marry. He had met a Princess, and the wedding was shortly to take place. But here he was now, preparing to make Angelina his wife. Perhaps this was triggering some inner turmoil that was being acted out in his dreams. Like all marriages, it would require some major changes for both of them. Was he worried that he would lose his independence, and no longer be "king" in his own life? Was he protecting himself from this perceived loss by maintaining an alternative persona in his imagination?

After several minutes Mel began to feel somewhat calmer. So it had all been a dream after all—but a very lucid one at that. He had once read that, during the lighter stages of sleep, our minds have the opportunity to free-wheel and create any sort of fantasy scenario they wish. Sometimes these dreams are triggered by recent events we have seen or experienced but, most often, it is something to do with our emotions.

A satisfying answer came to Mel. His mind went back to the boozy dinner date the previous night, when they had discussed what they each of them might come back as if they were reincarnated. This must have still been in his mind as he drifted off to sleep. His brain had then used these ideas to concoct the crazy story about him being Melchizedek, an important royal character from the past.

If he related this to anyone with appropriate psychiatric qualifications, that person would then have enough clinical data to sustain an entire conference with his academic colleagues. No doubt he would be told he had an ego complex, delusions of grandeur, suppressed religious yearnings, plus many other symptoms. He joked to himself that the experience of playing the lead role in his dream might have cured him of any desire to repeat this in real life.

Confident that, once he had washed, dressed, and had his first cup of strong coffee, the still persistent images of his nocturnal adventure would have all but disappeared. Feeling a bit itchy, Mel thought that a nice hot shower was the first thing on his "to do" list; perhaps this would help to wash away the memory of his dream, as well as refresh him physically. He went into the bathroom, turned on the taps, and took of his night clothes. Stepping into the shower cubical, he caught a glimpse of himself in the mirror. The serpent scales on his chest reflected back at him!

"Psoriasis," said the doctor. "This skin disease can take several forms, but yours is rather atypical. How long have you had it?"

"I had not noticed it before today," replied Mel. Despite this being a Sunday, and with an important meeting and lunch with his fiancée and future parents-in-law, he was so shocked by his physical state that he had immediately telephoned the emergency doctor. Luckily, he had managed to secure an appointment for later that morning. Then another call, this time to Angelina, saying that he was sorry but he would be a bit late for the chat. He fabricated a half-truth excuse that he would have to first call at the hospital because he had slipped in the shower and was worried he might have broken a bone in his foot.

"The causes of this condition are not always obvious," continued the doctor." It may be excessive smoking or drinking. Does either of these apply to you?"

No," said Mel, "I don't drink a lot, but maybe just had one too many last night."

"Well have you had any injury to the skin on that part of the body, perhaps an insect bite, or been overdoing the sun bathing?"

"I am not aware of any such damage, and I usually use sun protection," he replied.

"That only really leaves us with a psychosomatic origin," the doctor said. "Have you been under a lot of stress lately?"

"The only thing I can think of is that I have become engaged, and the wedding date is not too far off. Maybe I am wondering if it is the right time to settle down, and am also worrying about finding a house, along with the work that goes with setting up a new home. All this means borrowing a lot of money and having to pay this off for most of my working life." Mel was intentionally exaggerating his level of anxiety, in the hope that this would convince the doctor. To tell him what might be the true origin of his skin condition would most likely result in skepticism, and possibility outright laughter.

"Could this result in enough stress to trigger the psoriasis?" he asked.

"Possibly," replied the practitioner, "But it is still most unusual for such a condition to develop so quickly."

"Can you cure it?" was Mel's next question.

"Sometimes these things cannot be permanently cured," was the response, "But we can certainly try to treat it. I suggest a three-pronged attack."

"What do you want me to do?" asked Mel.

"I shall give you a prescription for a steroid-based cream. You could also buy an ultraviolet lamp and sit in front of it for fifteen minutes, at least twice a day. Then you will have to try and reduce your stress level—and make sure you cut down on your drinking."

"Thank you, I shall do as you say," Mel responded. "How long will it be before the scales fade away?"

"Difficult to say" replied the doctor. "You said that the condition came on suddenly, so maybe it will disappear equally as suddenly. But some cases never do completely clear up."

Mel left the surgery and made his way to Angelina's house as quickly as he could. Whilst not feeling very reassured by the doctor's prognosis, he nevertheless resolved to obey the instruction to stay as calm as he could. When he arrived, only half an hour late, everyone wanted to know about his foot injury. He had almost forgotten that he had used this as an excuse, but managed to continue the lie by saying that it was only a bruised bone, and nothing was broken. No doubt one day he would have to tell the truth to Angelina, especially if the psoriasis did not clear up, but now was not the time to do so.

The conversation turned to the matter of the wedding and, for the first time that day, Mel started to relax. He was with the girl he loved, and there were important decisions to be made. The church and the reception venue had been booked some time ago, so what remained was to agree on the guest list and the food and drink that would be served at the wedding breakfast. Angelina's parents appeared to have already made most of the decisions, although Mel made sure that his own friends and relatives would be included among the invitees.

It would have been nice if the couple could have moved into their own house, immediately on return from their honeymoon. Although they had seen several properties that appealed to them, no decision had yet been made, so they would have to start their married life in Mel's small flat. However, they resolved to try and find a new home as quickly as possible, once they were back.

With the discussion over, they made their way to a gastro pub for a leisurely Sunday lunch. Mel had decided that he must tell the others about the dream he had experienced the previous night. He did not want to risk accidentally making some reference to these events, and then have to frantically think of an explanation. This had already happened when he and Angelina met in the coffee shop, and he had inadvertently uttered the word "Salem." He then had to claim that this was the name he was thinking of for their new home together, once they had found a suitable place to live.

Mel began, not very originally, "I must tell you about this dream I had last night."

The others made a polite effort to show interest, suspecting that this will be just another example of a story that means little to anyone else but the teller. "I had somehow been transported four thousand years back in time, and met famous people like Noah and Abraham. I ended up being King and High Priest of Jerusalem."

His future in-laws and bride-to-be did their best to hide the amusement that this description must have generated. Angelina's father was the first to comment. "I am no Sigmund Freud, but don't dreams sometimes bring to the surface desires and aspirations that usually remain hidden? Perhaps you feel that you aren't very important, and have a desire to be a powerful king."

Although her mother nodded in agreement, Angelina spoke up in Mel's defense. "I don't think that is true; he has never come across to me as having such delusions of grandeur. What is interesting is that, when I met him in the coffee shop the other day, he appeared to be daydreaming about a place called Salem—the old name for Jerusalem." Turning now to her fiancée she asked, "Could your dream be prompted by some deep religious yearnings?"

The impact of Angelina's question certainly registered with Mel. Before this moment, he had not considered himself to be particularly religious. However, now that this point had been raised, he could see that it might be behind many of the thoughts and dreams that he had been experiencing recently. All he could manage to reply was, "That is an interesting suggestion, Angelina. I wasn't aware that I had any special interest in religion, at least not one deep enough to trigger dreams. I shall have to think about this some more." With that, the conversation moved on to other topics, but it left Mel in a rather pensive state of mind.

There was much to do before the wedding. The time went by quickly for Mel, and all the activities left him with little opportunity to give serious thought to whether or not he might have been developing strong religious aspirations. The scales on his chest, diagnosed by the doctor as psoriasis, were showing only a small improvement, despite being treated by the medication he had been given. The suggestion that the cause may be psychosomatic was becoming more likely, but he could not identify any worries except those that were to be expected with all the preparations necessary for his marriage.

The eve of the wedding soon arrived. Mel and Angelina went through the check-list together. Church ceremony rehearsed, reception arrangements completed, wedding dress and bridesmaids' outfits delivered, suits hired for the groom and best man, final list of guests confirmed, honeymoon bookings received—the list seemed never-ending. They each still had packing and other preparation to do on their own so, after an early evening meal together and a final fond embrace, they returned to their respective homes.

Once he was back in his flat, Mel busied himself with what he had to do. This would be the last night he would spend alone here, so he made sure the place was clean and tidy for when they returned from their honeymoon. A good night's rest was in order so, once his chores were complete, he allowed himself a last nightcap to help him settle down, and then retired to bed.

Mel closed his eyes, hoping that sleep would come quickly to save him from the mental turmoil that sometimes invaded his thoughts when he tried to relax. At last he felt himself drifting off into dreamland, but then became aware of a still, small voice whispering, "Melchizedek, please come back, we need you."

At once, all the memories of his other existence that were being suppressed came flooding back. It was clear that he could not continue like this, living in two worlds, but had to make a once-and-for-all decision.

He wrestled with the choice facing him. On the one hand, being a King and High Priest was an honor granted to few people, although it would require him to live in an ancient world, devoid of all the benefits that had been achieved through the advancement of science and technology. He would have to dedicate his life to making the city, and the world beyond, a better place. But he would have Queen Aushead by his side to support him and, hopefully, their progeny would establish a line of succession that would ensure the contribution he had started would continue.

On the other hand, he was due to marry Angelina tomorrow. He could look forward to a long-lasting, loving relationship, a family, and the joy of building a home and career. Of course there would be a price to pay, in terms of an expensive mortgage, the responsibilities of bring up children, and the compromises that went with both parenthood and the need to remain in stable employment.

Mel assumed that, if he did allow himself to be transported back in time to resume his priestly role, the opportunities to return to the present would be gone for ever. His lifeless body would be found when the police broke into his flat, after being alerted by his fiancée that he had gone missing, and was not responding to her telephone calls. Would the subsequent post mortem examination reveal the serpent scales on his chest, and the beginnings of horns and a tail, or would they have disappeared once his spirit had departed? If they remained, then Angelina would no doubt be relieved that she had not married what she would think was the devil incarnate.

He continued to anguish for what seemed like hours, but was probably only minutes, over the decision he inevitably had to take. He knew he could not continue with his present duel, schizophrenic, existence any longer; he had to concentrate on living just one life, and doing it properly. With growing confidence, but not without some regret at what he would have to leave behind, he came to his decision.

The voice spoke to him again, although it now seemed more distant than before, as if it were fading away for ever. "Melchizedek, we need you."

"I'm coming," he replied.

REINCARNATION

Mel's marriage to Princess Aushead was a joyous occasion, and it was warmly welcomed by the people of Salem. It was a happy union which, in time, produced two sons and a daughter, thus ensuring that the Melchizedek royal line would continue. The governance of the city, and the duties of High Priest, both still required wise and skilful management. Limiting expenditure to avoid a budget deficit was more difficult than had been anticipated, and it required a scaling down of some projects that were intended to improve Salem's infrastructure. Although there were spasmodic raiding parties, the strengthened defenses and the regular army were successful in repelling them. Whenever Mel doubted that he had the necessary ability to deal with a difficult situation, once again divine guidance came to help him.

The years passed. Mel realized that his physical appearance indicated he was growing older, but somehow he felt to be timeless, as if he would live forever. Despite some earlier prophesies that had suggested this, he still thought it was more likely that he would just die when his allotted time came, as did every other mortal being. Several remarkable and unexpected changes had already occurred in his life; would there be any more, he wondered?

Sure enough, fifty years after Mel had first entered Salem, Archangel Michael came to visit him again. "Melchizedek," he said, "Your mission in this place is now complete. You have fulfilled all that was required of you, and El Elyon is well pleased. It is now time to leave."

Many questions flooded into Mel's mind. "Where are we going? What will the people say if I suddenly disappear?"

Before he could continue, Michael interrupted. "We are going to heaven, where you will rest for a while before beginning your next assignment. Your appearance now is that of an old man. I shall come for you tonight, and we shall begin our journey; your lifeless, physical body will remain on the bed. The people will not be too surprised that their elderly king has died in his sleep. You will be remembered with affection at your funeral, and your name will be revered for many years to come."

Mel was starting to feel rather uncomfortable about what would shortly happen to him. He asked: "But what will be left of me when I leave this earthly body—will I just be a formless spirit?"

"Have no fear," replied the archangel. "If you wish, your spiritual self can look and feel just the same as your present physical one, but it will be ageless and immortal. When you are born again, your appearance will take on a new form."

Feeling only a little calmer on hearing this, Mel said, "You mentioned my next assignment, and now you state that I shall be born again. What is going to happen to me?"

All Michael would say in reply was, "I cannot answer your questions. When He is ready to do so, El Elyon will let you know what your future holds."

Mel dearly wished he could call together all his close friends and staff, tell them what would happen to him, and say "goodbye" to them. However, Michael had asked him not to reveal this to anyone, but to just let those who found him the next morning believe that he had died naturally of old age. Although he had agreed to obey these instructions, he did not want to just coldly abandon the woman whom had been his loyal wife and Queen for nearly fifty years.

Aushead was, like Mel, now showing her age and was no longer very mobile. Her once jet-black hair was now pure white but, to him, she remained the same beauty that he had married all those years ago. During what only he knew would be their last evening meal together, they reminisced about all that had happened to them since they first met. They had enjoyed a happy marriage, and produced three healthy children. Life had sometimes been difficult, but they had stayed together and overcome every obstacle.

Trying to sound philosophical but casual, Mel said, "We are not getting any younger, my dear, and one day we shall depart this earth. But we shall be content in the knowledge that our legacy will continue through our children." His wife was a little puzzled by such a statement, but attributed it to the second goblet of wine that he had drunk. Because of her mobility problem, Aushead now slept downstairs in what was originally the private office and dining room. Before retiring to his own bed upstairs, Mel embraced his wife one last time, and told her that he loved her.

Weary now, despite the drama that was to unfold, he was glad to lie down and try to rest.

"It is time to depart." Archangel Michael's voice broke the silence. "If you are ready, climb astride my back and we shall leave this place." Mel confirmed that he was prepared for what was to happen.

As they rose gently above the bed, he looked down at his now lifeless human form lying there. It had served him well, and he was sad that this episode had to end in this way. Michael had anticipated this and said, "Although the people will not know it, your body will disappear from the grave after being there for three days."

The Palace and the whole of Salem were quickly left behind them, and very soon Mel could see nothing of the earth at all. They had entered a dark, featureless void.

"Where are we now?" Mel asked.

"We have left the universe that you know," replied Michael. "There are many parallel universes, and the one we have now entered is the exclusive domain of Heaven."

Mel did not expect such a profound explanation. "But we have only been travelling for a very few minutes. How have we managed to already leave the earth and its universe behind so quickly?"

The Archangel seemed amused by this question. "Time and space only have meaning in the universe you had inhabited until less than one earthly hour ago. Where we are now, a million kilometers are but a centimeter, and a thousand years are no different from a second. We can travel to the beginning of time, or to the end, just as we wish."

Confused, but not wishing to display his ignorance, Mel remained silent and instead concentrated on what was going on around him. The inky blackness was slowly lightening and, far in front of them was a tiny point of blue light. Without being prompted, his companion said, "We are on our way to the Godhead, the primordial energy source that created all things. But we shall not be able to approach right up to it. No one is permitted to see the Supreme Being and live. Instead, we shall stop at a respectful distance, and receive details of your next assignment from El Elyon."

Once again, asking questions seemed inappropriate at this time; the momentous nature of the situation was overwhelming, and Mel needed to be able to assimilate all that he had been told. As it grew a little brighter, he could see that they were passing though streams of particles that were radiating from the central light source. They glittered with all the colors of the rainbow, and in some hues that he had never seen before. It was not empty space any more. There was also a sound all around them, a sound so exquisite and ethereal that it could not have been created on the world that he had previously known. [45]

He was filled with a sense of overwhelming joy and peace, and stretched out his hands toward the colored particles that were moving past him, hoping to catch some so that he take a closer look at them. However, although they gently touched his skin like tiny raindrops, they then just seemed to pass right through him and continue on their outward journey, evading capture. Michael then spoke again, once more anticipating the question that he was about to be asked. "This journey can be completed in an instant, or it can take a long time. Remember that we are not constrained by the physical laws that you were used to on earth."

Mel had no wish to quickly end the wonderful state of bliss he was now feeling, and wished for it to continue. "Please do not bring this trip to a sudden end, Michael, but let me savor the experience a while longer."

The Archangel was content to let the journey continue. As they travelled ever closer to the blue light, which had now become a shining orb, Mel started to see images of people appearing briefly in the space around him, before fading away again. Some of them looked familiar; folk he had known in the past—family members and friends who had now died. When he recognized someone, he tried to call out to them, and he saw their mouth move in response. Despite hearing no sound, the words entered directly into his mind. Everyone he spoke to in this way expressed joy at seeing him, and gave assurances that they themselves were in a perpetual state of peace and contentment.

"I see that you are reuniting with old acquaintances," Michael said. When we have reached our destination, you will have plenty of opportunities to rest, and to meet your friends before your next task. Princess Aushead will be among them."

Mel's joy at hearing this was quickly dampened by a thought that invaded his mind. "That will be wonderful, but it will be sad to see everyone as old people, just as they would have been when they died."

His companion was quick to reassure him. "You are still being influenced by the passage of time that you were used to on earth. In this eternal spirit world, it does not have the same meaning. You can be as old or as young as you wish, and your companions can appear to you as being of any age you choose them to be."

With this latest revelation, Mel's euphoria was complete. "This is indeed a wondrous place," he said. "I feel unworthy to be granted such a privilege when I have done so little to deserve it."

"The same experience comes to all people who come here," said the Archangel. He then added, "But those who have not been faithful to El Elyon take considerably longer to arrive than you did."

This prompted Mel to ask another question. "If this has been, and will remain, the final destination for all the people who have ever lived, why is it not already overcrowded?"

"Indeed, this is something that puzzles many people from earth," Michael replied patiently. "We are all formless souls or spirits, and we take up no space. We can adopt whatever form we please but, ultimately, we all remain a part of the Godhead that created us, and the size of heaven remains the same."

As the light grew ever brighter, Mel could see more distant images. There were utopian landscapes that reminded him of the Garden of Eden, but there were also lands, animals and plants which, though equally as beautiful, were alien to him. He could only surmise that there were inhabited worlds other than the one he had known, and that these were also represented in this wondrous place. Wherever he looked, there was color and a radiance far in excess of that which he had left behind. He knew he could never tire of gazing at the wondrous vista that surrounded him.

Archangel Michael eventually announced that their journey was about to come to an end. They had approached the shining orb that was the Godhead as far as was permitted, and were now setting down on the ground. Looking round him he saw familiar-looking trees and flowers, and could even smell the delicate perfumes of the fragrant blooms as they were carried toward him by a gentle breeze. Mel was sure that this had been created just to help him feel homely. By way of confirmation, his companion explained that, in this place, everybody perceived themselves to be in an environment where they could feel comfortable and at peace.

"You may stay in this place until it is time for you to undertake your next task, or you can travel anywhere you wish except toward the orb that is the source of all there is and will be. If you disobey this instruction, then your whole existence will come to a permanent end."

"I understand," confirmed Mel. "There is much to see and many people to meet. I know I shall be happy to stay here as long as I am required to do."

"Very good. We must now await instructions from El Elyon about your future assignment. I shall leave you to explore your new home, but I shall be with you again when the word comes from our Lord." With that, the Archangel left, and Mel had the opportunity to take a closer look at his surroundings.

Superficially, everything had an air of familiarity about it, and he felt to be just the same flesh and blood as he had always been. But was this all an illusion? There were many people in this place from all over his own world and, apparently, other worlds that were alien to him. From what Michael had said, everyone was made to feel happy and comfortable, so there must be a great number of different landscapes represented here.

What would he see if he went on a journey around heaven— would his own scenario move with him, or would it suddenly change as he entered the domain of people who preferred a different environment? After much careful thought, he decided it was most likely that everything that was visible was only in the eye of the beholder. Each person would see what they wanted to see. There could not even be any solid ground to support anything that appeared to be living and growing. The people here were no longer made of flesh and blood, but were made to feel so in order to retain a sense of selfhood. It was, as Michael had made clear to him, totally a spirit world, but a wonderful one at that. He would be happy to stay here as long as was necessary.

Whilst Mel was planning to explore, to see if his theory was correct, his Archangel friend returned to tell him that he would now learn what was in store for him. El Elyon began to speak. Although the voice was powerful, it did not come through the air, because there was no air in this universe. Instead it was projected straight into the minds of both of them, in whatever language they wanted to hear it. The message began, "Melchizedek, you have achieved well in your mission in Salem. With you I am well pleased."

This was nice to hear, thought Mel, but what would his future role be? He did not have to wait long to find out. "You will rest here for two thousand of your earth years. Then you will be born again to an earthly mother, not far from your previous home in Salem. You will learn the trade of a carpenter. Once again the people will have turned against me and started to worship false gods. There you will preach my word and promote my name as the one true God."

Mel's first reaction was that he would largely be continuing where he had left off in his previous mission. He was sad to hear that the good work he had started in Salem would not be maintained indefinitely, although he felt confident that his previous experience would help him to succeed again. But what El Elyon said next instantly banished any feeling of compliancy that may have been forming in his mind. "The people will turn against you, and your body will die a painful death. This will demonstrate your humility and dedication, and it will release your spirit so that you can return to me in heaven."

Now this inclusion of a painful death was not welcome news, but he hoped that he would have the necessary courage to go through with it when the time came. As if reading his thoughts, which of course he was, El Elyon added, "Do not fear, my son, I shall be with you every step of the way. You will return to me in glory."

This brought some comfort and reassurance to Mel, and he pledged to remain as brave as he could no matter what befell him. El Elyon had yet one more missive to convey. "Your work will still not be over, and there will be yet another task for you. After a further two millennia, you will again return to the world that you know. It will be the Second Coming, long anticipated by the faithful. You will have a normal birth, grow into a fine young man, and train to be an architect. Then the Badge of Priesthood will come upon you, and you will devote your life to furthering my kingdom on earth. As always, I shall be there to guide you." [46]

Once Mel had absorbed the impact of this latest revelation, the total picture became clear to him. He would be the same person in three incarnations, fulfilling El Elyon's long-term plan. This explained why he had suddenly started to develop the scales on his chest, and the small lumps that could grow into horns and a tail. It would mean that he would not be found dead in his flat on the day of his wedding. Did this also mean that his marriage to Angelina would take place after all? If this were the case, then he would have to explain everything to her. Would she understand, and stand by him during the years of his assignment? [47]

El Elyon had ended the conversation, and Archangel Michael had departed after saying that he would return to transport him to earth when the time came. Mel was left alone, happy and at peace with his thoughts. He lay down to rest, and to contemplate the life that lay ahead of him, but he soon lapsed into sleep.

He was again awakened by the sound of a telephone ringing. A telephone in heaven? Surely not. He picked up the handset and identified himself, "Mel, this is George, your best man," said the caller. There was a trace of anxiety in the other's voice. "You have taken a long time to answer, and I was worried that you had suddenly disappeared. I shall be around to take you to the church in an hour. We don't want to keep Angelina waiting, do we? You better be ready!"

APPENDIX

Notes on Supporting Evidence

CHAPTER 1: THE REBIRTH

(1) In his lecture entitled *Space and Time Warps*, Professor Stephen Hawking stated that the feasibility of time travel depends on whether or not we can make space-time so warped that we can go back to the past. He also mentioned Quantum Theory and that, if we can warp space-time in a negative direction, we may be able to construct a wormhole that will enable us to travel back into our past. http://www.hawking.org.uk/space-and-time-warps.html (Accessed 10th February, 2017).

(2) The Old Testament Apocryphal text, *The Book of the Secrets of Enoch*, was written by an Hellenistic Jew, around the beginning of the Christian Era. Section III, verses 17–19 states: "And when they had gone toward the grave, a child [Melchizedek] came out from the dead Sopanima and they saw the child sitting beside [her]. Noah and Nir were very terrified with a great fear, because the child was fully developed physically, he spoke with his lips. And behold the badge of priesthood was on his chest." (Morefill, W. R., and Charles, R. H., trans. Oxford: Clarendon, 1896).

(3) Another source indicates that the 'Badge of Priesthood' was a large patch of scaly skin. There could also be horns and a tail, and a tough hide-like skin. LeVesque, T. A. L. *The Ancient Ones* http://www.bibliotecapleyades.net/sumer_anunnaki/reptiles/reptiles61.ht (Accessed 11th February, 2017).

CHAPTER 2: THE ARK

(4) Genesis Chapter 5 reports the ages of Adam and his descendents, including Noah. The story of the ark and the flood is contained in the three chapters that follow.

CHAPTER 3: THE ARCHANGEL

(5) *The Book of the Secrets of Enoch* (ibid), Section IV states that the Lord instructed Archangel Michael to take Melchizedek to Eden to protect him from the flood.

(6) Daniel, chapter 12, verse 1 refers to Michael as the "great prince who protects."

(7) There are two main theories for the location of the Garden of Eden: the north (in Turkey), or south (presently under water in the Persian Gulf). The present narrative is based on the southern location. http://www.israel-a-history-of.com/biblical-garden-of-eden.html#VisitorPages. (Accessed 25th February, 2017).

(8) "Salem" was Melchizedeck's city. It was founded in the fourth millennium BCE. van der Crabben, Jan, 2011, http://www.ancient.eu/jerusalem/ (Accessed 13th March, 2017). It is generally held to have become known by its current name in the middle of the third millennium BCE.

CHAPTER 4: THE GARDEN

(9) Michael Grant explains that "Adam" in Hebrew refers to humankind in general terms. "Eve" may symbolize "the mother of all who live." The Garden of Eden was an idyllic oasis, "such as might have been glimpsed by early immigrants from the desert." *The History of Ancient Israel*, page 98. London: Weidenfeld and Nicolson, 1984.

CHAPTER 5: SALEM

(10) Michael Grant (ibid. page 101) states that "Floods of a Mesopotamian scale were not to be expected in Canaan."

(11) The similarities between the story of Melchizedeck and Jesus Christ are not mere coincidences. Gnostic scripts dating from the fourth century CE propose that the two are manifestations of the same person. (Nag Hammadi library, The Coptic Gnostic Library Project, accessed on-line 13th March, 2017). This is supported by Hebrews (5:5–6) "God said to (Jesus), 'You are my Son; today I have become your Father . . . You are a priest for ever, in the order of Melchizedeck."

(12) *The Book of the Secrets of Enoch* (ibid.), Section III states the names of the High Priests who preceded Melchizedek.

(13) Michael Grant (ibid. page 11), refers to waves of invaders entering Palestine. On page 19 he provides some demographic details of ancient Jerusalem (Salem).

(14) The description of Salem is based on a map "Jerusalem in Old Testament Times" in *The Holy Bible, Good News Edition*, Bible Society of South Africa, page 332, 1985.

CHAPTER 6: CONFUSION

(15) Carl Jung wrote about the persistence of memory in reincarnation. He noted that the concept of rebirth implies the continuity

of personality, and that one is at least potentially able to remember that one has lived through a previous existence. See: Jung, Carl G. *The Archetypes and Collective Unconscious* (page 201). Trans Hull, R. F. C. Princeton, NJ: University Press, 1959.

CHAPTER 7: THE KING

(16) Food and meal times in the Old Testament are were described in http://biblestudytools.com/encyclopedias/isbe/meals-meal-time .html (Accessed 12th April, 2017).

(17) Details of ablution practices, including the availability of soap, are revealed in a range of historical resources.

(18) The description of Melchizedek's clothing is based on artist's depictions, including an image of him painted onto the side of the altar, near the Royal Doors at Libotin wooden church, Maramures County, Romania.

(19) Michael Grant (ibid. p. 19) states that one of the governors of ancient Jerusalem wrote to the Egyptian pharaoh asking for troops. In return, the Canaanites could offer murex (a purple dye), oil, wine, ivory, cooking pots, and wood.

(20) Historical records mention several pharaohs by the name of Mentuhotep, with the second, third and fourth spanning the dates from 2060 to 1991 BCE. These dates are likely to coincide with those of Abraham, and therefore also Melchizedek.

CHAPTER 8: THE HIGH PRIEST

(21) Archaeological evidence for the design of ancient Canaan temples is reported by Wiener, Noah. *Bible History Daily*, 2016. http://www.biblicalarchaeology.org/daily/ancient-cultures/ ancient-israel/early-bronze-age-megiddos-great-temple-and-the-birth-of-urban-culture-in-the-levant (Accessed 25th April, 2017).

See also University of Pennsylvania Museum: *Canaan and Ancient Israel* https://www.penn.museum/sites/canaan/CanaaniteTemples .html (Accessed 25th April, 2017)

(22) Michael Grant (ibid. p. 22) mentions that the early Canaanite religion was Polytheistic, because of the difficulty in accepting that a single deity was responsible for the complexities of the universe. Ba'al was one of the false gods.

(23) The *Dead Sea Scrolls* (11Q13) state that Melchizedek will deliver the captives from the power of Belial, the devil.

(24) According to *The Book of the Bee* (Wallis Budge, Earnest A, ed. and trans. 1886, reprinted 2011, Oxford: Clarendon), chapter XXI, Noah's son Shem forbade Melchizedek to offer up to God offerings of beasts, but only flour, olive oil, and wine.

(25) Grant (ibid. p. 14) states that the Canaanite leaders were fortifying their small capital cities.

(26) The rabbinic text *Seder ha-Dorot* quotes Melchizedek as being the first to initiate and complete a wall in circumference of the city of Salem. https://en.wikipedia.org/wiki/Melchizedek (Accessed 2nd May, 2017)

CHAPTER 9: PROGRESS

(27) A description of the duties of Mesopotamian priests is given in: Anonymous, *Mesopotamian Priests and Priestesses* (Sep 19, 2014) http://www.historyonthenet.com/mesopotamian-priests-and-priestesses/ (Accessed 30th April, 2017)

(28) See note 15 concerning memories of a previous existence

CHAPTER 10: ABRAHAM

(29) Some details of Terah's life are given in *Parashat Lech L'cha* by Rabbi Joan Farber. http://wupi.org/Publications/Newsletter.asp?ContentID=484 (Accessed 8th May, 2017).

(30) Leon Wood mentions the polytheistic nature of the religion in Ur, including worship of the moon-goddess Ningal. He comments on the Abraham story in Chapter 3, *A Survey of Israel's Ancient History*, Grand Rapids: Mich: Zondervan (1986, p.19).

(31) Details of the journey of Terah and Abraham, the visit to Egypt, and the rescue of Lot, are described in Genesis chapters 11–14.

CHAPTER 11: PHARAOH'S REPLY

(32) Records show that an Egyptian nobleman, Hannu, lived during the time of Pharaoh Mentuhotep.

(33) Grant (ibid, p.16, 18) describes how some of the Canaanite cities were fortified.

(34) Deuteronomy 31:4 mentions the defeat of the Amorite Kings Sihon and Og by Joshua, and Joshua 2:10 states that they were killed. Melchizedek's imagined encounter would have been before this, and Sihon fled after he was defeated.

CHAPTER 12: WARRIOR KING

(35) Descriptions of early warfare are given in *Ancient Egyptian Battle Tactics* (2012), https://owlcation.co./humanities/Ancient-Egyptian-Battle-Tactics (Accessed 8th June, 2017).

(36) Evidence that he was destined to be a warrior comes from *Melchizedek*, Nag Hammadi Library. "Be strong, O Melchizedek ... for the archons (leaders) who are your enemies, made war (but) you have prevailed over them—and you destroyed your enemies." The same document frequently refers him as the "Priest of the God Most High."

(37) Genesis 14:17–22 describes the meeting with Abraham, the tithes and the refreshment. This is the first time that tithes are mentioned in the Bible. Blessings are given by a superior to an inferior,

and tithes are given by an inferior to a superior. Thus Melchizedek was superior to Abraham. http://www.generationword.com/notes_for_notesbooks_pg/hebrews/7_1.htm. (Accessed 22nd June, 2017).

(38) The expression "a priest for ever" is stated in Psalm 110:4, which then adds, "in the line of succession to Melchizedek." It is repeated several times in Hebrews chapters 5, 6 and 7. *The Book of Enoch* (Appendix, p. 29) reports the Lord telling Nir that Melchizedek will be a "priest of the priests for ever."

CHAPTER 13: FEMALE COMPANY

(39) Although *"zedek"* is from the Hebrew meaning "righteousness," the mention of King Adoni*zedek* in Joshua 10:1, 3 can lead one to fantasize that he was an off-spring of Melchi*zedek*.

(40) Princess Aushead was indeed Pharaoh Mentuhotep's daughter. Images depict her as a black woman. It is not known whom she married.

(41) Joshua Mark outlines traditions relating to wedding practices in Mesopotamia (2014) and in Egypt (2016) in *Ancient History Encyclopedia* http://www.ancient.eu/article/688 and 934 respectively. (Accessed 28th June, 2017).

(42) Robert Naranjo gives some details of the Mesopotamian marriage procedure. See: *Marriage in Ancient Mesopotamia and Babylonia*, E-History, The Ohio State University. https://ehistory.osu.edu/articles/marriage-ancient-mesopotamia-and-babylonia. (Accessed 12th July, 2017).

CHAPTER 14: THE PRINCESS

(43) The descriptions of the royal barges, what the princess might have worn, and what the richer Egyptians ate, are based on historical evidence reported on several websites.

CHAPTER 15: THE PROCLAMATION

(44) The Jubilee Year is described in Leviticus 25:8–55, including proclaiming liberty throughout the land. Melchizedek is not mentioned there, but he is in the *Dead Sea Scrolls* (11Q13, Col.2). This fragment includes the statements: "the inheritance of Melchizedek," and "the "Year of Melchizedek's favor." These imply that he instigated the Jubilee, and that it continued thereafter.

CHAPTER 17: REINCARNATION

(45) There are many accounts of people claiming to have out-of-body experiences. These were consulted to inform the present narrative, including *Proof of Heaven: A Neurosurgeon's Journey into the Afterlife*, by Alexander, Eben. New York: Simon & Schuster, 2012.

(46) The book of Hebrews contains one of the very few references to Melchizedek. Chapter 6, verse 20 reads, "Jesus has entered on our behalf. He has become a high priest for ever, in the order of Melchizedek." This reflects a similar phrase stated in Psalm 110:4. (See also note 38, vide supra).

(47) For other elements of this chapter, see above note 1 (the notion of time warps), note 11 (similarities between Melchizedek and Jesus), and note 15 (Jung's notion of memories of previous existences persisting in the memory).